Sangria in the Sangraal

or

Tucked Away in Aragon
(The Albarracín Tales)

by

Rhys Hughes

Sangria in the Sangraal
by Rhys Hughes

Publication Date: September 2016

Copyright of the text of **Sangria in the Sangraal** lies with Rhys Hughes, 2016.

Cover and Interior Art by David Rix, copyright 2016

ISBN: 978-1-908125-43-9

www.eibonvalepress.co.uk

Dedicated to
Olga Zolle

and
all my Spanish friends

CONTENTS

9   *Author's Foreword*

13   The Shapes Down There

21   The Spare Hermit

31   Sally Forth

39   The Magic Gone

53   Oranges and the Arrows

61   The Man Toucan

71   Latitude, Longitude and Plenitude

81   The Kind Generosity of Theophrastus Tautology

91   Scaramouche's Pouting Mouth

101 Knossos in its Glory

109 Señor Chimera's Hysterical History

121 The Bone Throwers

Author's Foreword

I discovered the small city of Albarracín purely by chance in late summer of the year 2007. I was living in Spain at the time and living as cheaply as possible, for I had very little money. Walking everywhere was one of my habits and I would spend days and weeks camping wild in the mountains. Already I had hiked across the Alpujarras and Sierra Nevada to Granada and was now looking for new horizons.

I was aware that the Tajo is the longest river in Iberia; the trickle that snakes through Aragon hills crosses into Portugal and becomes a gigantic mouth in the Atlantic littoral. I decided to find the source of the Tajo. An arbitrary choice but it finally led me to the most picturesque town I have seen in Spain, and yet a place strangely unsung. Two weeks I lingered in the rosy ancient environs of Albarracín.

Each night I slept in the mountains far above the crumbling walls and towers; every day I descended to solve another mystery. Almost as soon as I arrived I guessed I would write a cycle of stories set here, and I knew those stories would be very strange, fey and infused with the otherworldly character of old Albarracín. I suppose that the book I had selected to carry on my expedition also partly inspired me.

A masterpiece of interlinked narratives and a fine example of the 'Gothic' literary movement of the late 18th and early 19th Centuries, Jan Potocki's *The Manuscript Found in Saragossa* is as intricate and chaotic and wondrous as any Arabian Nights' entertainment, but the complete text wasn't published until long after the death of its remarkable author. For many years only a set of ten tales were generally available.

Perhaps in late symmetrical homage to this sombre fact, my own miniature cycle of 'Spanish tales' originally featured ten stories too. But for this second edition, the one you hold in your hands at this precise moment, I decided to write two new stories, extending the sequence both into the future and into the past. Fortunately, twelve is a number with as many symbolic and mystical associations as ten.

Albarracín hides itself in the most obscure and depopulated corner of Spain. From space at night, this region is still mostly devoid of lights: on the ground it has a curiously unchanged aspect. There are many Neolithic cave paintings lost among the limestone crags and bubbling springs. With the exception of interior Sardinia, no other southern European landscape feels so removed from the talons of Time.

Rosy walls, rosy mountains, rosy clouds: Albarracín!

The Shapes Down There

High above the formless mass of seething humanity, the clouds go about their business, seemingly oblivious to events far below. Clouds always have work to do, giving visible substance to the winds, topping up rivers with rain, securing the privacy of mountain summits. At least that's the impression they like to give each other. The truth is that idle souls come in all shapes and sizes and can even be found in the heavens.

"Daydreaming again! But I thought you were supposed to be helping with the late afternoon rainbow?"

It was a stately Altocumulus lenticularis who spoke these words but the young Cumulus humilis to whom they were addressed merely said, "I'm sure I won't be missed. There are plenty of other clouds available for that task. I prefer to gaze at the ground."

"You won't succeed in atmospheric society if you keep doing that," objected the Altocumulus. "Staring at land all day won't help you at all."

The younger cloud shrugged. "I don't care."

At this the Altocumulus sighed and replied, "When I was your age I also went around with my head in the clods of earth. So I do understand the appeal. Tell me, do you see shapes down there?"

The Cumulus humilis nodded. "Many shapes. I sometimes wonder if humanity possesses some sort of conscious will and arranges itself deliberately into startling representations of celestial objects?"

The older cloud laughed at that. "You talk like a child sometimes. 'Humanity' is not really an integrated phenomenon but is composed of thousands or even millions of individual particles called 'citizens'. I don't enjoy spoiling the poetry of your imagination with science but I studied sociology at college and know what I'm talking about."

The small Cumulus chose his words with care. "All the same, the similarities to real things are often remarkable."

"Yes, they are. I'll give you that."

The Cumulus nodded in an absent minded way and redirected his attention at the ground. It was a beautiful summer day. The towers, battlements and houses of Albarracín blended in so well with the landscape that no join or hint of discontinuity was discernable. And separate streams of humanity were now winding along the steep streets of the town, clattering over the cobbles and converging in the main square, forming a quivering mass.

"Look there, at that amorphous blob!" cried the Cumulus humilis.

"The correct, technical term is 'mob', but we'll let that pass," asserted the Altocumulus lenticularis.

"Don't you think it looks like a nebula?"

"Almost," reluctantly conceded the elder cloud, "but it depends on your personal psychology, and we should also take into consideration the particular nebula you might be referring to. The night sky is full of them and each one has unique characteristics, so I can only offer you a conditional agreement."

"Sometimes I wish you would lighten up," said the young Cumulus.

But the Altocumulus took serious offence at this remark. "Lighten up? You need a stern lecture on the facts of meteorological life, my boy! I'm not a simple convection cloud like you are, rising on thermals generated by the sun-warmed ground, but an orographic cloud, formed when the winds are forced up over a range of mountains and the water vapour they carry is cooled by the subsequent drop in air pressure. In other words, I'm *already* lighter and higher than you'll ever be!"

"I didn't mean it that way," stuttered the Cumulus humilis.

But the Altocumulus lenticularis wasn't in a mood to be appeased so easily. "My altitude is approximately twice yours…"

"Yes," replied the younger cloud ironically, "and that means I'm closer to the ground and thus in a better position to accurately perceive definite shapes in the mobs. Now I can see a pair of comets on a collision course! And over there, to the right, is a Cumulonimbus anvil! It looks just like a friend of yours, all gloomy and bombastic."

"Just a coincidence and not even a significant one," snorted the Altocumulus lenticularis. "You ought to spend your time in a more productive manner. Staring at the ground all day will turn you daft. Optical illusions have no value at all."

The Cumulus humilis instantly rejected this advice. "But they *are* important! The question for me is always: why? Why do solid things down there so often mimic the objects in the sky? A trick of nature or something more profound? Could it be possible that messages have been encrypted in the billowing crowds that circulate daily over the landscapes beneath us?"

"That is all arrant nonsense!" gasped the older cloud.

"No, it's not. I mean, you can't be *certain* there isn't something in what I say, can you? For instance, consider that little knot of citizens at the foot of that tower. Don't you agree it resembles a gibbous moon?"

"Yes, for a moment, but now it's breaking apart and has become shapeless again. It's purely a matter of statistics. Combinations over time..."

But the Altocumulus lenticularis was suddenly interrupted by a newcomer. So animated had the conversation grown that it was attracting the attention of other clouds. "What are you looking at? Trying to find patterns in the lower chaos, eh?"

"Yes we are," answered the Cumulus humilis.

The newcomer was a Cirrocumulus lacunosus undulatus and he floated so high above the other two that he had to shout to make himself heard. "I sometimes do that as well..."

"But it's a waste of time!" cried the exasperated Altocumulus.

"Not at all, not at all," replied the Cirrocumulus. "I consider it a superb way of relaxing the mind before engaging myself in more serious tasks. It's almost a form of meditation."

"That's it exactly!" babbled the Cumulus.

"What shapes have you seen so far?" asked the newcomer.

"A nebula, two comets, the moon and even a storm cloud. In fact I can see another cloud now!"

"Where is it?" demanded the Cirrocumulus.

"Between the fortified wall and the house with the red shutters. It looks just like a Stratus nebulosus translucidus!"

"Ah yes, I can see it too!"

"Bah!" huffed the Altocumulus.

The commotion was attracting more and more clouds and some of them even beckoned to their friends over the horizon. Soon the sky was packed with all species and varieties of cloud, including some Nacreous and Noctilucent types, generally twilight or night clouds, that had been woken up by the din.

"This really is intolerable," grumbled the Altocumulus.

"What's going on down there?" cried the latest arrivals. "It looks as if the humans are throwing a party! See how they converge along all those streets into that large open space in the middle of those buildings? Almost as if they're up to something! You don't suppose a riot is on the way, do you?"

"Gentleclouds, please disperse!" pleaded the Altocumulus.

But they weren't prepared to listen to him. Suddenly one small point far below grew brighter and the clouds gasped with amazement and pleasure. "How delightful! They are forming a representation of the sun. They nearly seem intelligent sometimes…"

"Superstitious fools," muttered the Altocumulus.

The emir of Albarracín stroked his beard and the rings on his fingers reflected the firelight as he did so. His name was Hudayl Djalaf 'Izz ad-Dawla and he had ordered this blaze in the *plaza* as a crucial part of the general festivities. Albarracín was now a sovereign nation, small but perfectly viable, and today was the very first day of his reign, so he had decreed an entire week of frivolity and games to celebrate the newly declared independence of his state.

He smiled as he regarded his subjects from his balcony. Soon he would go down to join them, but first he wanted to enjoy viewing them as a single mass from afar. Gathered in concentric circles around the immense bonfire, his citizens personified the waves of heat given off by the sun. As for the real sun, that was setting now, and the long shadows of the towers were melting into the slopes of the hills on which they rested. Soon his people would be dancing for him under the stars and he would move among them, nodding and laughing.

The stars? He glanced up at the sky and frowned. There would be no starlight tonight. Where had all those clouds come from? Never in his life had he seen such a strange mixture of cloud types. Was this an unlucky omen? It would be a big disappointment if rain extinguished the fire and curtailed the first night of freedom for his tiny and remote principality. But there was nothing he could do about the weather, so he finally shrugged and decided to join the main bulk of his subjects.

Down the stone steps he went and along a narrow passage to a door leading onto the street. The ambassadors from Alpuente were passing at the time and bowed respectfully as he stepped out onto the cobbles. Alpuente was an even smaller kingdom than his own and had already been independent for three years. Hudayl Djalaf 'Izz ad-Dawla greeted the ambassadors and walked with them to the central square. He had no need of guards because nobody hated him. Nobody on the face of the Earth.

The sky was a different matter. Perhaps the clouds had mistaken his love of liberty for arrogance? But no, the rain still didn't fall, and in fact it seemed those aerial masses of moisture were losing interest in his fiesta. They began to disperse in different directions, clearly indicating the presence of crosswinds high above the mountains. By the time the emir reached the fire in the *plaza*, only one cloud was left up there, a small puff of dark wool that blotted out less than half a constellation in the now glittering night.

Musical instruments twanged and wheezed and dancing feet stamped the cobbles in merry rhythms, but the concentration of Hudayl Djalaf 'Izz ad-Dawla was entirely captured by the blaze before him. He ignored all other demands on his attention. The blazing logs crackled and spat and the resulting embers seemed to form transient shapes in the middle of the greater glow, the outlines of dragons and other mythical beasts. At one point he thought he saw Albarracín itself, with towers and walls of fire, ringed by burning mountains and overlooked by fiery sunset clouds. He laughed and shook his head.

Then he looked up. The solitary cloud was still there.

*

Deep within the formless mass of seething flames, the embers go about their business, seemingly oblivious of events all around. Embers always have work to do, creating and chasing shadows, taking the edge off the chills of night, giving visible substance to the winds by ejecting showers of sparks. At least that's the impression they like to give each other. The truth is that idle souls come in all shapes and sizes and can even be found where the fire is hottest.

"Daydreaming again! I suppose you see shapes out there? I do understand the appeal. When I was young…"

The Spare Hermit

He wore a hooded grey cloak and a pair of *esparto* sandals and carried a staff in his right hand and an unlit lantern in his left. He was a penniless traveller but nobody who met him on his journey said, "You look like an illustration on a Tarot card!" because clichés hadn't been invented yet. Nor had Tarot cards: another reason.

Incidentally, the first cliché was created by accident in the workshop of an incompetent alchemist in the 16th Century, five hundred years after our story begins. Alchemy doesn't work, so only the bad alchemists ever produce anything of value or potency.

Not that a cliché has value. But all the same…

Incidentally again, when I say "our story" I don't really mean it's yours as well as mine; I was just being polite. The earliest Tarot cards date from 1430, though some mystics insist their origin goes right back to Ancient Egypt. The name of the traveller was Murk. He had spent his last coin the previous day and was utterly destitute.

He had only the belongings that filled his large pockets: a small knife, a piece of flint, a few husks of coarse bread. Originally from Toledo, he had been expelled for a minor offence involving the drunken daughter of an important official, and now he was walking roughly east towards the tiny independent nation of Albarracín.

He was almost at his destination, having just reached the small spring that is the ultimate source of the Tajo, the longest river in Iberia, the same one that flows through Toledo in fact, though he hadn't closely followed its meandering course. The Tajo reaches the sea where Lisbon stands and has an immense mouth there, but here it was small enough to scoop in a cupped palm and be sucked dry by greedy lips. The same holds true for every river, so don't be too surprised.

Having slaked his thirst, Murk stood and continued his wanderings, though the sun was starting to set behind him. If he walked all night, he would reach Albarracín before dawn. He planned to offer his services as an adviser to Abu Marwan 'Abd al-Malik, the second emir of that curious realm, for it was well known that his city-state required wise men to defy the expansionist designs of Zaragoza.

In the heavy red beams that slanted all around, the red rocks and earth of the mountains seemed to glow unnaturally, like the soles of sore feet, and a sudden tiredness descended on Murk. The road wound up and down across the hushed landscape and was rarely smooth; around the next bend it hugged the base of a crumbling cliff.

He turned the bend and yawned. Then he blinked. A cave gaped by the side of the road and in front of the cave sat an old man on a large stone, drawing circles and ellipses in the dust with a long stick. He looked up at the sound of muffled footsteps and squinted. Then he stood slowly with a smile and pointed with his stick.

"Greetings stranger! What's your name?"

"It's Murk," called Murk.

"A coincidence! My own name is Lurk!"

"That's not exactly the same, is it? It's not truly much of a coincidence, but greetings in return anyway!"

"Thanks. You are headed to Albarracín? I must warn you that the road between here and there is infested with robbers. Even if you are penniless they'll assault you and break your bones. Force of habit, I guess. Don't go further in this direction. Seriously!"

Murk regarded the old man suspiciously. How could he be certain this advice wasn't some kind of trick?

"What should I do then? I must reach the city!"

It seemed that the old man had been anticipating this question, for he started to reply even before Murk had finished asking it. "I like the look of you and so I'll let you in on a secret," he whispered, "and that's the fact that this cave actually leads to an underground passage that surfaces at a point *beyond* the robbers. If you walk along it to the very end, you'll be able to avoid the rogues completely."

Murk was dubious. "I'm not sure. I don't like enclosed spaces and I'm scared I might get lost. It'll be pitch black and slimy inside. What if I fall and bash my skull on a stalagmite?"

The old man said, "You have a lantern, don't you? Use that to generate beams. What could be more simple?"

Murk opened his mouth but found that he didn't have any arguments to fill it with, so he closed it again and removed the flint from his pocket and struck sparks with his knife and lit the wick. Then with the lantern aglow he entered the cave mouth. The old man named Lurk shouted a few words of encouragement after him. The cave didn't widen at all but sloped down at a gentle angle like a castle corridor.

Yet this wasn't an artificial structure, for the walls were studded with crystals that sparkled as he moved towards them, the orange of his flame creating green, purple and blue flashes of ethereal colour on the facets of each gem. The passage continued to descend and Murk supposed he was walking straight through the mountain.

For an hour he kept up a jaunty pace, then he slackened somewhat; but he didn't stop to rest, for he wanted to emerge in the fresh air as rapidly as possible. He was suffering from a tinge of claustrophobia and hoped the passage would start to rise soon, but in fact it continued to slope down at a very low angle, yet he reasoned that it still couldn't be too deep, for the pressure in his ears wasn't painful.

Maybe I can divert your attention for a few moments to point out that the Tarot card known as 'The Hermit' is associated with the characteristics of introspection, silence, guidance, reflection, solitude, distance and deep understanding. The word *deep* is probably significant here. Some say that the symbol is a Threshold Guardian who represents an obstacle that must be overcome, one that also integrates all the lessons of the sunlit world. I cribbed this from an encyclopaedia.

By the time my explanation is done, Murk felt a cool breeze waft over his face and knew he was approaching the end of the tunnel; but this was a disturbing fact, for he still hadn't ascended so much as an inch to make up for the sloping down. Maybe Albarracín was at a lower elevation than the source of the Tajo? But it's not.

Was he approaching a cavern full of wind?

Back then, in the 11ᵗʰ century, it was commonly supposed that winds slept in caverns when not blowing.

Not this time. This breeze was a free one.

Murk stumbled forward, emerged from the cave mouth he had entered, the very same one. The landscape was identical; the sun was still setting. The only difference was that the old man had gone. Lurk was nowhere to be seen and the circles and ellipses he had scratched in the dust were gone too. It was a bitter disappointment.

"The liar! I'm no closer to my destination!"

Murk extinguished his lamp with a petulant puff, sat on the stone that had served Lurk for a chair. Too glum to continue his walk, he imagined that a long rest would suffice to reinvigorate him, but he didn't have much opportunity to discover the truth of this, for abruptly a fellow appeared from around the bend in the road.

"Greetings stranger!" cried this man.

"You are the stranger, not me," pointed out Murk.

"Come now, you're supposed to ask me my name. You have to follow the rules, otherwise it's not fair."

Murk studied the stranger closely. He wore a hooded grey cloak and a pair of *esparto* sandals and carried a staff in his right hand and an unlit lantern in his left. "No," he said.

"No! What do you mean?" gasped the stranger. "My name is Durk and I'm travelling to Albarracín to volunteer as an adviser in the service of the emir, Abu Marwan 'Abd al-Malik. This cave is where you live, yes? You are a hermit, a wise man? Truly."

Murk shook his head. "To play a joke on a pauper is most undignified. As if life isn't already hard enough!"

"It's not a joke," hissed Durk, "but a restructuring."

"This madness is unbearable!"

"Now you must warn me against proceeding down this road. Tell me about the robbers that infest it. Encourage me to enter this cave mouth and walk along the subterranean passage to the end. Then I'll emerge in the next world and it'll be *my* turn to be the hermit. That's how matters can be most efficiently arranged."

Twisting his mouth into a grimace, Murk cried:

"If I can't go forward because of robbers, and I daren't go back in the direction of Toledo, and I can't bear to stay and listen to your nonsense, there's only one thing I *can* do!"

And he jumped off his stone and hurried back into the cave, pursued by Durk's curses. He groped his way in darkness for a few minutes, then paused to relight his lantern. Although weary in the extreme he forced his legs to keep moving, and in fact the further he went the more energy he seemed to accumulate. Bizarrely the slope went down again all the way and he emerged in front of the same cave mouth, where he extinguished his lantern and sat on the stone.

Not more than a few seconds later, a new stranger appeared, but Murk ignored him. The stranger huffed.

"What's the meaning of this? Aren't you going to ask my name? I am Surk. Aren't you going to warn me about the robbers that infest the road ahead? Aren't you going to persuade me to enter this cave to bypass the villains on my way to Albarracín?"

Murk didn't look up. "No."

"But you *must*. There are rules to follow."

"I refuse, I refuse!" roared Murk. Then he stood and began running in the direction of Albarracín, despite his blisters and the ache in his joints, his staff held before him like a lance, his lantern swinging like a mace, while Surk shook a fist at his back.

"Don't break the sequence so soon! Come back! There are robbers on the road! *Especially* if you are penniless they'll assault you and break your bones. Force of habit, I guess."

Murk paid no heed and loped in an ungainly fashion.

Surk watched him go until he was lost to sight, then he discarded his own staff and lantern, picked up a long stick, sat on the large stone and drew circles and ellipses in the dust.

The hermit has internalised the lessons of life to the point that he *is* the lesson. Withdraw at the wrong time, stay withdrawn too long, and growth stops. The hooded cloak the hermit wears protects him and isolates him. At some point he must cast it off.

Cast it off and rejoin the world. More cribbing.

Murk slowed his pace to a trot, then found himself passing a shelter cut into the rotten base of a thick tree. The sun had finally gone down, a thin moon was up, but he wasn't able to see the top of the tree, and the noise he made alerted the sleeping occupants of the shelter, who rushed out half dressed, with rusty swords.

"Stop! We are robbers! You must not pass!"

"Rather disorganised, aren't you?"

"We weren't expecting you just yet. Everything's still at the rehearsal stage. Give us all your money!"

"I don't have any. Not even one coin."

"Penniless? In that case you can pay off your debt by permitting us to cast you down a deep well. My name is Krum, by the way. Don't worry, you'll be cast down *gently*. Kindly step into this large bucket and remain there. Otherwise we'll kill you!"

Murk wanted to protest, but at the tip of a sword, even a blunt one, he was disinclined to make a big fuss.

The lip of the well was formed of misshapen logs and Murk climbed over it easily enough and squatted in the bucket, undulating in unhappy rhythm while the robbers worked the windlass and lowered him down the vertical shaft. The walls of the pit seemed made of rough bark that flaked away at the touch of his fingers.

A wooden well? He reached the bottom.

There was no splash of water. The base of the well was dry. Dim light shone from behind a thin partition. He vacated the bucket and pushed his way through a tattered grimy cloth…

And emerged at the front of the shelter again!

The well had been the inside of an immense hollow tree, the same tree that contained the shelter. But that wasn't possible! It made a mockery of space and direction. He stood among a group of dishevelled robbers who were staring and nodding at him.

"Where is Krum?" he cried.

"Who? There's nobody around here with that name. My name is Krul and this fellow is Krud. We were told that our new leader would arrive out of this tree. So that means you must be him. But you've come early, if you don't mind me saying so."

"I can't be your leader. I've never been a robber before and I wouldn't know how to fulfil my duties!"

"Simply wait for the next traveller who comes along this road. Then capture him and lower him down the well to the very bottom. That's your task. It's extremely easy. But there might be rather a long wait before anyone new comes along this road. The hermit positions have to be filled first, *then* the robber chiefs. There are dozens of worlds to colonise and organise. A complex business!"

Murk shook his head in anguish. Then he fled down the moonlit road in the direction of Albarracín.

"Don't be so selfish!" shouted Krul.

But Murk didn't even look back. He pressed onwards until the walls of Albarracín were visible at last. Only a few lights flickered in the highest buildings, for the hour was late.

A sleepy guard occupied an alcove in the wall.

He noticed Murk and extended his pike. "The city gates are shut until the morning. My name is Lorb. You must turn back now and if you don't I'll be compelled to lock you up!"

"But I've walked so far!" objected Murk.

Lorb evidently decided that this utterance constituted a refusal to obey his instructions, so he moved out of the alcove, jabbed the traveller with the tip of his pike and ushered him to a narrow door set into another part of the wall. Keeping his pike point in contact with the lower spine of his captive, he said in a rough whisper:

"I'm going to lock you in here for the night. You ought to step meekly inside, for if you attempt to run I'll hurl my pike at you. I can use it like a javelin and I'm a very good shot."

"Understood," croaked Murk.

"Good. What's your name? I bet it's Torb or Gorb?"

"Neither is even close."

"Hmm, what about Horb, Korb or Porb?"

"I'm afraid not. Sorry."

Lorb shrugged and jabbed Murk through the door, which he then shut and locked with a large rusty key. It was dim inside the cell. Murk rattled the bars of the door to no avail. Then he turned and walked to the far end of the cell. Before reaching the far wall, he almost fell down a hole. A pit in the middle of the floor!

It was too dark to see anything. On his hands and knees he felt for the edge of the hole and quickly realised it wasn't a pit but a stairway and that this was the highest step! Where might it lead? Slowly he began to crawl down, descending in a tight spiral. There was a faint chance that freedom existed at the very bottom.

At last he reached the final step.

A dead end? He felt along the walls and everywhere else. There was a circular hatch in the floor, unlocked. He swung it open. Weak light, fresh air and assorted night sounds…

He lowered himself through the hatch and dangled by his long arms in mid air. His feet were still a few inches above the ground, so he let go. He found himself standing in an alcove; he stepped forward and the walls of Albarracín loomed around him.

A pike was resting on the floor, waiting for him to pick it up and adopt the role of guard. Next to the pike were a chain mail jacket, a dented iron helmet, a bunch of keys. He stooped and picked up the keys, trying each one in the lock of the main gate.

Finally the massive lock turned and the gate creaked open. At last he was within the city! Even fewer lights burned than before in the windows of the houses. He went to look for a warm place to sleep. Without money he couldn't expect to stay in a proper inn, but surely a comfortable stable existed somewhere nearby? He followed his nose up a narrow alley. Yes, there was a small stable this way.

Another man was already slumbering on the straw. He opened his eyes at the sound of Murk's approach and said, "You're very early. My name is Brog. Are you Brol or Brok…?"

Murk never learned the truth of the situation.

The simple fact is that the many different versions of Albarracín were spares. It's such a lovely city, you see, a perfect gem. Too fine to be lost to fire or war, so spares were created.

Maybe it's the only city with backup copies.

And every city requires a context, so the surrounding countryside had also been duplicated, the mountains, forests and rivers. And there had to be real sky, rather than a roof of rock.

But a city without a population, without commerce, without *life*, isn't worth keeping, even in reserve; and that's why all these Albarracíns had to be filled with appropriate citizens, with merchants and bakers, soldiers and scholars, even with robbers and hermits, for a city without soul is as useless as one without buildings.

If the Albarracín on the surface was destroyed for any reason, the one just below could be brought up to replace it, and if *that* one was destroyed the next one below could be brought up. And so on…

Murk lost count of all the levels.

The deeper the level, the less populated the Albarracín. It would take a great many generations to fill them all.

One fine morning, the second emir of the city-state, Abu Marwan 'Abd al-Malik, happened to glance out of the highest window of his citadel and he frowned deeply at what he saw.

A figure dressed in a hooded grey cloak and a pair of *esparto* sandals, who carried a worn staff in his right hand and an unlit lantern in his left, was wandering the citadel courtyard as if he belonged here. He must have let himself in with his own key.

The emir sighed. Changes to city life were inevitable now. For one thing, there would be less privacy.

The population had doubled overnight.

Sally Forth

"Hey, you down there! What the hell do you think you're doing, casting a grapple through my window?"

"Never fear, fair maid! I won't fall."

"You don't actually intend to climb up here, do you?"

"Verily and it won't take long."

"I don't like intruders or salesmen. Go away."

"Impossible! I know my duty. I've read the code of chivalry. The last page was missing, true, but I guessed the ending. You are a damsel and need rescuing. I must rescue you!"

"That's rather presumptuous, don't you think? Stop climbing the walls of my house at once. You are damaging the stonework with your heels, to say nothing of the vines. Desist!"

"Alas and alack, fair maid, I suspect that an enchanter put those words into your mouth and that you are under an enchantment. The enchantment of an enchanter! The worst kind!"

"I'll cut the rope with a pair of scissors!"

"Not this rope, I'm afraid. This rope is a hollow rope and inside it is an inner rope woven from iron wire. It's cutproof. Besides, you are not just a damsel but one that falls into the specific category of *rescuefiable*. I have no choice but to rescue you. None."

"What word is that? I know it not!"

"None means less than one but more than minus one."

"Not that word, the other word!"

"Minus, you mean? Minus means… Well, it's an abstract concept from India, difficult to put into words."

"Not *that* other word, the word in italics."

"Ah! Perhaps if I hyphenate it, all will become clear. Rescue-fiable. In need of rescue, able to be rescued."

"Did you make it up yourself, I wonder?"

"I did. The word 'certifiable' was my model. I suppose I'll have to keep hyphenating it until it catches on."

"Hyphen-ate? What odd speech you do have."

"Aye, maid, for I am an English knight, newly arrived in Spain, forced to flee my own land for over-rescuing damsels. There are only so many, a quota if you like, that can be rescued before the rescuer incurs wrath and I exceeded my quota and thus incurred that wrath, cauldrons of it, courtesy of rival knights. I was self-exiled here. Anyhow, only recently did I learn the languages of Spain, namely Arabic, Mozarabic and Hebrew. I haven't bothered to learn Visigothic yet."

"Almost a dead language, that one is."

"Yes. Well, I arrived in Albarracín yesterday but already have rescued a giggle of damsels. They do come in giggles, don't they? That's the right collective noun, isn't it? I hope."

"I assumed they came in swoons, but grammatical details such as that aren't my strong point. Whether giggles or swoons, be advised that I will cry for help if you climb higher."

"But I'm not illicit, not a moonlighter. I did check with Yahya Husam ad-Dawla, the third emir of this city, if it was acceptable for me to rescue damsels within his territories. He said yes, and he was even persuaded to sign an affidavit as confirmation."

"Show me that affidavit immediately!"

"Nay, for I need both hands to climb this rope, as well you know, but the moment I haul myself through your window, I'll reach into my jerkin and extract the relevant scroll and unfurl it before your eyes. Then I'll get you out of those clothes fast."

"I beg your pardon? You'll do *what*?"

"Tear off your dress. With my strong hands. Cast it to the floor. Stamp on it with feet shod in metal shoes. Your dress is your oppressor and I am ready to deal with it accordingly."

"That is most unseemly! How dare you?"

"I dare because of my courage, which is partly genetic, partly a legacy of my training and partly a result of the ingestion of various herbal brews with a reputation for steadying the nerves, borage for instance, a flower of a brilliant blue hue. So I'm not only a courageous knight but a *borageous* one. That's my joke, I invented it."

"You are a common molester in my view!"

"By no means, fair maiden! I am doing my duty, no more, no less. The code of chivalry is unambiguous on this score. A damsel in a dress must always be rescued, no excuses."

"In *distress*, you mean. Not in a dress."

"No, no, I'm quite sure of the wording. I checked it carefully. A knight must be perpetually prepared to rescue a damsel in a dress. Any damsel in any dress. Every damsel in every dress. Logically it must therefore be the dress that is causing the anguish from which she ought to be rescued. No other explanation makes sense."

"And to complete the rescue, you divest the dress?"

"There's simply no other way."

"You divest with urgency and ardour?"

"I do. Thank you for understanding. I divest until the damsels are fully undressed, which is the only way of redressing the insult to their virtue. I divest until the damsels are clothed only in blushes. Some blushes reveal more than others; a few are strangely less revealing than clothes! That's a paradox that may repay research."

"This is all very intriguing, but…"

"But what? I am halfway up this rope. A 'but' at the halfway stage is a hazard almost equal to a fray."

"Your pun only works in English. Distress, in a dress. And we are in the tiny sovereign state of Albarracín where English isn't spoken; in fact we're not speaking English right now, which makes a gross mockery of the entire exchange; more to the point, the kind of English that a knight of the early 12th century would speak couldn't accommodate that particular example of wordplay, I'm sorry."

"I take your point. The objections you raise can't be sneezed away, and yet I won't permit them to distract me from my quest to snatch you out of that dress and expose your nudity."

"I do have another objection that isn't linguistic."

"Really? Tell me, if you will!"

"I must candidly state that I have already been rescued. By Sir Sponge of Lewisham, who also exceeded his quota and was self-exiled here last week. He too obtained a permit from Yahya Husam ad-Dawla for a batch of fresh rescuing in Albarracín."

"Sir Sponge of Lewisham! My archrival from the vicinity of London! A rusty loon! Did he divest you?"

"Yes. You can speak to him if you wish."

"Spare me that indignity!"

"Well, he's here anyway and wants a word…"

"Lookee there, it's Sir Mustard of Shoreditch. Archrival? Yes, ha ha! I bet you never thought to encounter me again, did ya? Tough luck, sonny. Been busy since my arrival, I have, divesting damsels of dresses. I doubt there's anything left for you, maybe just a few puffed sleeves or shoulder pads, but certainly no damsels inside 'em. Ha ha! What's that? You want me to show my face at the window? No chance, pal. I'm invisible. Got an opal wrapped in a bay leaf, see, which is a sure charm against being seen. Time to sling yer hook, matey."

"Villain! I shall finish climbing this rope and then challenge you to the mortal combat you deserve!"

"No fear o' that, chum. I'm sending you down."

"My rope is cutproof, oaf!"

"I may not be able to sever your rope, but the barb of your grapple has caught only in this cheese, which this damsel just left lying around, and a cheese may be sliced and sundered with a dagger. Like so! And now you fall back from whence you came. Goodbye, dork! See you at the bottom, sucker. Hasta la vista, booby!"

"Verily he plummeteth. Ouch!"

"Yes. He is bashed to bits at the base of the wall."

"Many thanks for your help, dear sister. Your impersonation of a rival knight was inspired. Truly."

"Was my English accent convincing?"

"Yes, yes, I believe so."

"He's the umpteenth foreign knight to arrive in Albarracín in the past month with an intent to rescue damsels in dresses. The emir really needs to tighten up the immigration laws. Otherwise we'll be overrun in a year or two. Who would have thought a time would ever come when a damsel didn't feel safe in her own dress?"

"Know what I say to the womenfolk of this place?"

"No, I don't. What do you say?"

"Once more into the breeches, dear friends!"

"Good advice. A damsel in trousers can't be said to be *in a dress*. But doesn't that pun only work in…"

"Hush! Don't pick holes. We might fall through."

"Fair enough. Anyway, it's a good job we have this useful guidebook to give us the lowdown on each knight that turns up here. Bought it in a charity shop, I did, and it was certainly a wise investment. Orderic of Sark's *Rough Guide to Heraldic Signs, the Knights that Sport 'Em, their Lives, Loves and Archrivals*. Lucky for us also that most knights insist on wearing surcoats displaying their coats of arms. We are thus able to turn their own vanity against them."

"Vanity is too strong a word. Coats of arms are an accepted custom. I don't think self-love's intended."

"Agreed. All the same…"

"Look down there. Someone's coming!"

"It's Yahya Husam ad-Dawla himself, out for his morning walk. He is pausing to bend over the dying body of the knight. They are exchanging a few words of wisdom or regret."

"Can't you overhear what they are saying?"

"My ears are acute but the knight is faint. Let me carve the rest of this cheese into a hearing trumpet… Now if I write each word down as I hear it, you can share the conversation…"

"Man from a distant land. Tell me please, why you lie there in pieces when there are many better things to do in my domains? There are horses to ride, flowers to sniff, lutes to pluck. Why not enjoy a nice steam bath instead of sprawling in dust?"

"I can't. Don't mean to be rude. I'm dying."

"Why is that, my friend?"

"I was told to sally forth by my calling and my conscience, so I sallied forth but it availed me not."

"How curious. You aren't the first to give that reply. Who is this Sally Forth? She must be a woman of unique charms to exert such a fascination over so many strapping men. A sultry and ravishing temptress, strangely unobtainable. And she lives here, in Albarracín! Perhaps I should marry her? Well, try not to leak too much on the cobbles. I'll come and see how you're getting on tomorrow."

"Getting on! Don't you mean going off?"

"Ha! That's the spirit! Humour in adversity. My state needs more men like you. Live ones, I mean."

"Thanks. Goodbye. I'll remain on my back and stare at the sky until the mortal coil is shrugged fully off. Look at that cloud directly above! Cumulus humilis, isn't it? Do you think it looks like an angel? Wait, it's changing! Now it's a teapot."

The Magic Gone

With a profound frown on his battle-scarred face, Pedro Ruiz de Azagra asked his minstrel, "Who's that fellow over there? The one with the blue shirt standing in the green corner."

The minstrel shook his head, squinted and said, "I have no idea. Never seen him in my life. Didn't you invite him? He can't be an impostor; you ordered a doubling of the guard at the gates. He must have come with the delegation from Toledo unless—"

"I wasn't introduced to him!" cried Pedro.

The minstrel rubbed his chin.

"Look," he said, "at his expression: dreamy and focussed at the same time! I don't think he has been inside a castle before; he is fingering the tapestries like a lover plucking at a damsel's skirts! Maybe he's practising for some show later: a jester…"

"Unless what?" demanded Pedro.

"I beg your pardon, sire?"

"You were about to offer an alternative explanation for his appearance in this chamber. You said, 'unless—' but you didn't finish the sentence. I crave to know the missing words."

The minstrel answered, "They are easily provided. I was merely about to suggest that maybe he was spontaneously generated there in that corner from the mould on the walls."

"Yes, it is rather a *green* place, isn't it?"

"Sire, we know that maggots are born in putrid meat; and boars, bears, wolves and weasels are hatched from snowballs in the mountains; so why shouldn't a fully-grown man coagulate from castle moulds? I wonder if I might make a song about this?"

Pedro lifted a bejewelled hand. "Later."

The minstrel bowed as the rings on the fingers scintillated in the warm flicker of the fire. "Tomorrow."

Pedro nodded. "Fetch him, good Bertran."

The minstrel, who was a mighty warrior in his own right, walked with a scrape of his long sword scabbard on the flagstones across to the figure in the blue shirt. He grinned in what he hoped was a friendly manner, but he knew from experience that people often recoiled at the savage sagacity in his eyes; yet this newcomer merely returned the smile and said, "Hello there! What year is this, please?"

Bertran de Born looked back over his shoulder at Pedro and mouthed the words, "Just a mooncalf…"

Pedro continued to frown; it suited him.

"Are you with the delegation?" Bertran asked the fool, though it wasn't conceivable the answer was yes. The Archbishop of Toledo did *not* travel with imbeciles in his retinue, but then it occurred to the minstrel that this man might have lost his senses *after* his arrival in Albarracín; such things were possible: a fall down some stairs, the bite of a wild animal, anything might ruin a sane human mind.

The blue shirt gleamed in the shafts of sunlight. "Somewhere between 1150 AD and 1190 I hope," murmured its owner anxiously. "The controls can't be more out than that, and yet this cloth isn't right. Visigothic design indicating the late 7th century…"

Bertran leaned forward. "It's an antique."

The man's pale eyes showed both embarrassment and relief. "Yes, of course! I forgot that the fittings and trappings wouldn't be contemporary with the present age – with *this* age – but would be older, a patchwork of periods; for men have always bobbed in a soup of styles, heirlooms rising and falling together with modern objects like potatoes and carrots in the domestic cauldron of any room!"

The minstrel peered over his shoulder again and mouthed, "He mixes his metaphors very badly. He's not a professional jester but a pretender. I think he might be Cerebrun's spy."

40

Pedro Ruiz de Azagra absorbed this information; he was still frowning and he refused to relax his visage for another full minute. The wild scar in the heart of his brow was Λ-shaped, a perfect representation of the Greek letter lambda, and if he frowned deeply enough it straightened out or even inverted into a Latin V, which he liked to think resembled a surplus smile higher than any smile ever before.

Then he made a decision and strode manfully over to his possibly less than innocent guest, his hands extended in greeting. "Welcome! Welcome to my humble abode, my castle!"

The blue shirt rustled. "Are you the Lord Pedro?"

"At your service, I am!"

"So pleased to meet you! My name is Harold Clatter and I am a visitor from another year: from a distant century. I came in a time machine from an institute devoted to historical research. I'm preparing for my doctorate, you see, and I need first-hand experience for my thesis. There are *gaps* in the records. The chaos of life—"

Pedro and Bertran exchanged glances.

The latter cleared his throat and said, "Good sir, you made a reference most arcane. We understand not."

"Did I?" blinked Harold.

Bertran de Born smiled. "Yes, you said the word 'potatoes'. Forgive us our ignorance of such terms. You are a scholar, a self-confessed man of learning, but we are simple knights. I flatter myself that I have some skill with the lute and the quill; but philosophy and the weirder arts of natural science go not gently into my ears."

"The same is true for me," said Pedro, "though my own fumblings at the lute are of no consequence."

Harold Clatter looked distraught. "I forget! I forget! It's not so easy to change one's *context* entirely, to adapt one hundred percent. Always there will be discrepancies, mistakes!"

Pedro urged, "Calm yourself, good sir!"

"I'll bring him wine," said Bertran, and he turned and fetched a tankard from a nearby table. "Drink up."

Harold sipped the liquid, smacked his lips.

"That's better, much better! I'm dishevelled in mind and body because this is my first voyage through time. It's expensive to rent a machine. For five years I took a part-time job in a warehouse as a watchman to save my fee. I have been so tired for years!"

"None of us may rest for long," said Pedro sympathetically. "Troubled times are here again to test us."

"As always! Yes, indeed! But different kinds of troubles, no? For you it is more visceral than for me…"

Bertran whispered in Pedro's ear, "He is talking scholar-speak again. I wonder if truly he works for Cerebrun? I think not, for the Archbishop is cunning enough to choose his spies more carefully. Ask him directly what he thinks of Aragon and Castile?"

Pedro nodded and gripped Harold's shoulder in his powerful hand. "It is a sweet afternoon outside, and the mellow light on the battlements is a purer gold than any in the coffers of the King of Navarre, and thus do we consider ourselves richer than states ten times our girth; yet Albarracín is threatened by jealous rivals and this evening we must play another round of the infernal *axedrez* with them."

"Against the Archbishop of Toledo," added Bertran.

"*Axedrez?*" frowned Harold. "Ah, chess! Power politics. Yes, I see. It's a metaphor, an accurate one too!"

"Lord Pedro mixes them not," Bertran said wickedly.

Harold was unaware of the barb. "It seems I've arrived at an awkward moment. I realise you are busy men. I was hoping for an interview with Your Lordship; that maybe you would allow me to consult your written records, converse with your people."

"My people are happy; I speak for them," growled Pedro.

Harold began, "Yes, but if—"

Bertran said, "Come now, sir, why maintain the bluff? We know thou art no jester, nor a mooncalf, but we are unsure if you are an agent of the ravenous wolves who wish to reduce this proud independent kingdom to a province of their own realms."

Harold opened his mouth in shock. "Oh!"

"What *are* you?" cried Pedro.

"But— I haven't lied! I'm a real student, a postgraduate from a century when the world is different, so different!" Harold felt beads of sweat rise like tiny mushrooms from the pores of his skin. He shook his head, flung many droplets over his hosts, but they didn't seem to mind at all. "I'm not *that* kind of spy, not the bad kind."

"What do you think of Castile? Of Aragon?"

Harold saw his chance. "It would be a disaster if either kingdom took over the state of Albarracín, which has been an independent entity since the year 1012 AD when the first emir took advantage of the downfall of the fabled Caliphate of Cordoba…"

Pedro Ruiz de Azagra stroked the hilt of the sword in its scabbard but not in a menacing manner; it was an automatic gesture, one that warriors are prone to making without thinking. "That is not entirely true, not all of it, my friend. Albarracín wasn't independent after the *taifa* collapsed in the wake of Yahya Husam ad-Dawla's disastrous reign. Then came devils from the lands of heat and lions to seize most of Spain and poke grievous holes in our hides, malign demons."

Harold clapped his hands in childish glee.

"Yes, yes! The Almoravids! They are partly why I'm here. The history of Albarracín has been researched extensively by other students: most of it is very well-known; the days of the Ancient Iberians, the Roman times, the Visigothic era, the rule of the Caliphate, the sovereign *taifa*… What's missing is the dark age of Almoravid control, almost fifty years, and also the early days of your own regime."

Pedro smirked. "Once I saw a face in the clouds that looked like you. Above the city walls it bobbed."

"I saw it too," said Bertran, "and fired an arrow at it."

"With my bow," added Pedro.

Harold swallowed. "Why shoot an arrow at a cloud?"

Bertran laughed ironically.

"To prove the futility of certain things," smiled Pedro. "Now I fear we have been wasting our time talking with you. I suspect this conversation is no less *futile* than trying to burst a cloud with a barbed shaft. We have important affairs of estate to deal with. You are our guest and the dictates of honour compel us to treat you in the style you deserve. There is a nice dungeon below for your use."

Harold Clatter took a step backwards.

He collided with a large spherical object, black and riveted, threaded with veins that pulsed gently.

"I swear I'm no liar! I'm a time traveller!"

"How does one prove such a fancy?" asked Bertran, turning to Pedro with raised eyebrows. The Lord of Albarracín held up both hands, palms facing upward, and sighed. Bertran nodded and said to himself, "There's no easy way, that's for sure."

"Wait, wait! Here, here!" screeched Harold.

He reached into the pocket of his jacket, removed a small cylindrical object, gripped it too firmly.

Pedro and Bertran focussed on it.

"A fire machine!" screamed Harold, doing something with his thumb. A spark jumped, then flame.

Pure blue tongue, wavering gently.

Pedro cried, "A magic tinderbox. 'Tis a wonder!"

"Aye, not bad," agreed Bertran.

"It's powered by gas, by inflammable air," stammered Harold, "and it's called a *disposable lighter*!"

Pedro held out his hand to receive it. Harold passed it to him. With an expression of anguish that he didn't actually feel, Pedro spun the toothed wheel with his thumb. Flame appeared. He dropped the cylinder in alarm, laughed at his own timidity and picked it up. Luckily it was undamaged. He tried again: another flame. He displayed it proudly to Bertran, holding it before his friend's hot gaze.

"A disposable," approved the minstrel.

"Odd name," commented Pedro. He conjured another flame into life, a fourth and fifth moments later. "But a good device, easier than steel, flint and shavings. Yes, I like this."

"We have them in my century," said Harold.

Bertran asked him directly, "Even if this proves you come from a time not our own, then still one question remains: *how* did you arrive here? To travel from city to city, state to state, is difficult enough an ordeal. But to pilgrimage across centuries..."

"No mule could manage that," said Pedro.

Harold was still pressed up against the black sphere. Its circumference was so large that its north pole almost scraped the ceiling of the chamber and the door that gaped open in its side was larger than a big shield. With slow movements, the student turned and rapped on the riveted metal with his knuckles. It clanged loudly.

"In *this* thing. It's a rented time machine!"

Pedro and Bertran looked.

They went pale; their eyes expanded.

Croaks emerged from their throats as they contemplated the mass. For a moment it seemed that Pedro was about to attack it with his bare hands and his teeth. Harold said, "Psychology explains why you haven't noticed it until now. It's too far outside your experience; it gave you instant blind spots when it appeared. Your eyes saw it but your brain rejected the data. That is a common phenomenon."

"So it's true. You *are* from another age."

"Yes, I am. And inside this machine I have plenty of other fantastical devices from my own time. For instance I have a small box that can fix images permanently and another that preserves sound without distortion and another that allows one to—"

Pedro reached out to pluck the sleeve of the blue shirt. His gentle tug almost dragged Harold off his feet. "Will you help us? Will you take our side against Cerebrun, the Archbishop of Toledo? He works for the King of Castile and also has the support of the Pope. Albarracín to them is an anomaly or thorn to be removed."

"A glaring example of independence," said Bertran.

"Of course I will!" simpered Harold. "That's one of the reasons I chose to write my thesis about this place at this time. Independence! Yes, that's what I have faith in too. Indeed!"

Pedro and Bertran nodded at each other.

"Excellent!" cried the former. "Then you must live here in accordance with your exact true status. This is a solemn promise I make to you. Help us defeat Cerebrun at the debate tonight and always your exact true status will be honoured in my domains."

"And I will compose a song about you," said Bertran.

Harold was overcome with emotion. "This is more than I expected and I don't know how to thank you!"

Pedro flung his arm around Harold's shoulder.

"Merely show Cerebrun and his retinue what you have. Make fire and other tricks. Talk about your own era. Stress that you are on our side, on the side of the Lordship of Albarracín," he said. "The meeting takes place tonight in the other banqueting hall."

Harold giggled. "You have two banqueting halls?"

"More than two. Three! Do I not deserve them? It was I who made this kingdom a Christian land. I did this with force of arms, a valiant heart and divine assistance. Now I have aid less divine, but remarkable nonetheless, for a less physically strenuous but equally hazardous endeavour! A visitor from a more heroic age *on my side*!"

Bertran produced a lute from somewhere; perhaps one was resting on a windowsill behind a tapestry. He plucked a soft chord and sang almost to himself in a language that was not Catalan, Castilian or Mozarabic. For half a minute, Harold tinkered with the translator in his ear: then he had it adjusted correctly again. The tongue was the *langue d'oc* of the Provencal troubadours and Harold remembered that it was a convention of the finest minstrels to compose their songs in only that language. Silver lute strings shimmered and he listened intently.

Pedro pretended to be embarrassed. "Ah, my friend exaggerates all my achievements! He too is brave; he too is honest! What have I done to win such fulsome praise? Too little!"

Harold saw that Pedro knew all the words by heart. The song was one that recounted his life in full: his boyhood in Navarre; his marriage to the sweet damsel Toda Pérez; his self-exile from his homeland after a king he did not agree with, Sancho VI, gained the throne; his career as a solider in the service of the clever and generous Muhammad ibn Mardanis, ruler of the *taifas* of Valencia and Murcia, who entrusted to the young mercenary the lordship of Albarracín in order to defend it against Aragon; his fervent zeal in this mission; the years spent Christianising his vassals; his refusal to acknowledge Toledo's supremacy.

There was blood and heat and heart and sparks in the lyrics. The clash of sword edge on shield, the dull thunk of mace on skull, the jab of spear point through chain-mail armour, the death screams of Aragonese soldiers as they were repelled at the gates.

And even though he concentrated with most of his mind on the song, it seemed to Harold that other words bubbled below the melody, the words of Pedro's recent promise to him:

"In accordance with your exact true status!"

Then the long song ended.

Pedro Ruiz de Azagra was radiant and said to Harold, "Always spoils me, does good Bertran de Born; and surely our history is pallid compared to yours? I'm aware of this fact."

Harold spluttered and waved his arms.

"No, no! I assure you; Albarracín has a marvellous history! That's why I came here in the first place! But there are things about it even you don't know. For example, there are other Albarracíns below this one; spares! It must be a fair exchange, I maintain, for you to give me all the information I lack in return for such snippets!"

Bertran scratched his head. "Spares?"

The concept was clearly too radical for him to absorb; as for Pedro, he hadn't heard Harold's odd outburst and while Bertran replaced the lute on the windowsill, he said to his guest, "The debate tonight will be a difficult one for me. Cerebrun has the authority of the Pope. To defy him may risk excommunication, so it is better to nudge the conversation from the topic at hand. I will introduce you as—"

"Plain Mister Harold Clatter will be fine."

"As you wish. Then you will approach Cerebrun and his men and talk about yourself, about life in your own period. He will be intimidated, and then he will be at a disadvantage."

Harold nodded. "How many hours do I have to prepare?"

Pedro smiled. "No hours at all."

Bertran explained, "The debate begins now…"

"But you said it was due to take place *tonight*," objected Harold. Even as he spoke these words, the light in the chamber dimmed and he realised the sun had gone down over one of the red mountains that ringed the city. Hidden in its narrow valley, Albarracín had a shorter day than most other parts of Spain. Into the hall came a sooty hunchback to light lanterns on the walls. Pedro and Bertran motioned to Harold to follow; out they went through the furthest door of the room.

Harold trudged after; the doorway disgorged him into another chamber almost identical to the first. But it was bisected with a long table where a dozen men already sat in a neat line.

Pedro Ruiz de Azagra bowed deeply, ironically.

Bertran de Born did the same.

"The magnificent Cerebrun, Archbishop of Toledo!" announced Pedro as he turned to face Harold Clatter.

"With his acolytes and knights!" added Bertran.

Cerebrun raised a languid right hand. A ring of enormous size seemed to weigh it down; his jowls shook with the effort. The other men perched next to him began slamming their empty goblets on the table surface in an intricate rhythm; this was the music of fanaticism and suppressed fury. It was difficult for Harold to focus on it. He trembled and felt the fingers of Bertran in the small of his back.

Prodded into action, Harold cried, "I am—"

"Magus Harold!" boomed Pedro.

Harold gasped. "*Mister*."

"Tell him the truth! Reveal who you are!" growled Pedro.

"Time traveller!" croaked Harold.

Cerebrun studied him intently, turned to his nearest companion, arched his catastrophic eyebrows, muttered something. The companion mumbled in return, frowned, stroked his beard.

"From a more heroic age!" continued Pedro.

"Show them!" urged Bertran.

Harold fumbled with his lighter, dropped it, picked it up again, turned the toothed wheel with his thumb, then sparked into life a drunken flame that was quite impressive in the thickening gloom. He held it as steady as possible until it scorched his flesh.

The flame died instantly. Pedro smirked at Cerebrun. "Ask anything of him! Anything! He's a prodigy!"

"From another age in time!" stressed Bertran.

The Archbishop consulted with the companion on his other side. Then he nodded and spoke directly to Harold, his voice deep but not rich, jowls keeping time with his syllables:

"Tell me about Troy! About the wooden horse!"

Harold swallowed. "I don't know anything about that, I'm afraid. I was hoping to talk about my own age."

"Yes, yes! Tell me about Romulus and Remus!"

"I know very little about them."

"Then speak of Cleopatra and Caesar!"

Harold laughed a hollow laugh. "Again I must disappoint you. I'm not from the past but the future and—"

Cerebrun began laughing: his companions too!

Harold said, "But the future has greater marvels in it than the Classical world. Let me tell you about auto…"

Something jerked him backwards; he felt an enormous crushing force around his neck. It was the arm of the Lord of Albarracín! Tiny points of light filled the corners of his vision and the Archbishop and his acolytes blurred into a meaningless stain of colour. He was dragged out of the hall into the other chamber and flung on the flagstones. He gagged, rose to his knees, looked up. Pedro and Bertran sneered down at him, both fingering the hilts of their heavy broadswords.

"Dog! You deceived us!" screamed Pedro.

"No, no!" protested Harold.

"You have embarrassed us and made our task more difficult. Cerebrun now has the upper hand," said Bertran.

"What did I do wrong? What?" gargled Harold.

"Everything," sighed Pedro.

Bertran leaned forward and hissed bitterly, "You are from the *future*, not the *past*! We assumed you were from the past. You didn't warn us! Everyone knows the past was a better time, when men were stronger and cleverer; and women were lovelier too. Mighty heroes lived in the past but now we just have middling ones. The race of mankind grows feebler every new generation: that's common knowledge. Achilles was ten times stronger than the most valiant crusader alive in our own day and he lived nearly twenty five centuries ago."

"Work it out for yourself," snapped Pedro.

"I can't!" whimpered Harold.

Bertran counted ostentatiously on his fingers. "Every two thousand and five hundred years we become ten times weaker. Therefore we lose one tenth of our strength every two hundred and fifty years. This means we lose one hundredth every twenty-five years, which is one generation. These sums are simple enough!"

"No, that's not right. It doesn't work—"

Pedro interrupted him. "What year are you from?"

Harold answered without thinking, "2066. Time travel has only been generally available since 2050."

Bertran counted on his fingers again. "That's eight hundred and ninety four years from now. Almost thirty-six generations. You are more than a third of a man weaker than us."

Harold said nothing; he blinked instead.

Pedro rasped, "I promised to house you here in accordance with your exact true status! I never willingly break a promise. Come with us, with good Bertran and myself, down."

"Down where? Down where?" shrieked Harold.

"Exact true status!" echoed Bertran.

They lifted him easily and carried him down a spiral staircase into the catacombs under the castle. Here were murky corridors, slime and bones. And doors that led to tiny rooms.

Passing one room, Pedro jutted his chin inside.

A ragged figure in the corner rattled its chains and gurgled; the gurgle was a laugh of madness. Rats scurried. Pedro said, "He was a mercenary from Valencia, leader of a band of swordsmen. A great fighter! His name was Louis the Wolf. Perhaps it still is. I do treat him like a captured wolf, for that is his exact true status…"

They passed along to another dungeon.

"And this one is for you," smiled Pedro, "but you are less than a wolf, so I will treat you like a dog! A mangy cur! Sometimes I will let you out for walks, throw you a bone."

"A good dog is two thirds of a man," explained Bertran.

"Sometimes," conceded Pedro.

Harold made no attempt to resist.

With the magic gone he was almost nothing.

A dog's life is a hard thing.

But it could be worse…

Back on the surface, in the first hall, Pedro nudged Bertran. "What to do with that thing? Any ideas?"

The minstrel studied the time machine. "If we saw it in half, sire, one hemisphere might be used as the dome of a building, and the other for a big cauldron in your kitchens."

"You are right, Bertran, as always. Right."

"Thank you, sire. I am."

Oranges and the Arrows

There are no orange trees in Albarracín.

Do you know why? It's because of something Fernán Sánchez did one fine morning on the walls of the city.

He fired an arrow at a stork passing overhead.

Let's hear about it!

Don Fernán was a young knight with an ailing mother, and because she seemed likely not to live much longer, he didn't go off to fight in wars in Outremer and other distant lands.

He stayed behind and looked after her.

But he was a warrior at heart and soon grew impatient with peace and soft living and he sought for something to distract his mind and discharge his warlike urges. It wasn't enough to brawl with his friends in the taverns after midnight; that was poor sport.

He taught himself the longbow instead.

Parading the city walls, he would take aim at targets on the other side, shooting wild animals. The taking of life was important to him; virtuosity in itself held little attraction. He was a knight, a killer. Before long he was an archer of surpassing deadliness.

Soon there were no foxes, boars or rabbits left alive within bowshot of Don Fernán's unfailing eye. So he turned to shooting birds down from the sky; he had heard that men in olden days riddled the clouds with shafts to make rain, but he thought that foolish.

He killed the storks that flapped heavily over the battlements; and for this he was summoned to explain himself to Baron Antonio, who sighed with exaggerated intolerance and said, "It was twenty eight years ago that Albarracín lost its independence, and since that time we have considered obedience to be the finest of virtues."

Don Fernán replied, "But I always conform—"

"To the whims of slaughter only!"

"With respect," said Don Fernán, "I am a frustrated knight and should be riding against the scimitars of Saracens in Palestine, not languishing in this infernal serenity; I keep my wits sharp as best I can. When monotony weighs on my spirit, I shrug it off."

Baron Antonio sighed again. "It alarms me that you impale migrating storks because you are bored. Don't you know that it's unlucky to kill this bird? They are symbols of kindness."

Don Fernán had an answer ready, for he had expected this interview in this chamber in these precise circumstances, and said, "The storks deliver unborn children to married couples, this is well known; some of them will be born in the lands of our enemies."

"Dear boy, that superstition is an idle fancy."

"Not so, my lord, for I have seen small bundles in their beaks with my own eyes, and I know the hordes of the infidels are multiplying. How can we forget the Kingdom of Granada, still ruled by Moors? Whenever I see a stork flying in *that* direction, I kill it. One less future soldier who might march against us when he grows up!"

"And if the stork is flying in some other direction?"

"I leave it pass in peace, truly."

Baron Antonio fidgeted with the hem of his robe. This was a ludicrous argument but an ingenious one and he had no retort. Finally he waved his hand and allowed the youthful archer to step free. Don Fernán returned to his house and to his poorly mother.

Doña Isabella was sprawled in her chair.

Her hair was dishevelled and her face was very pale; her hands shook, her eyelids fluttered. What was wrong? An empty bottle of wine rolled a hollow drone of misery under the legs of her seat and came to rest next to all the others with a dismal knock.

He felt her forehead with his hand. Still hot.

The finest doctors had come to see her; all had prescribed the solitary remedy that worked for every affliction. Red wine. Even Isaac the Jewish physician, who at first speculated that wine was the *cause* of the problem, changed his mind when Doña Isabella clawed at his throat and refused to let go. "Even if overindulgence is the root of the sickness, there is no cure other than more wine!" he conceded.

Don Fernán had implicit trust in that judgment.

So the wine continued to flow…

Once when Don Fernán was strolling his way to the city walls, Baron Antonio happened to pass him in the opposite direction, carried on a litter by men who were probably slaves. "Don Fernán! Your mother was once good to me; I want her to get well. Be aware that a person can be weaned off any poison, however sweet."

"Poison? There are assassins here, my lord?"

Baron Antonio shook his head. "Sometimes one is tempted to poison *oneself*, my boy. Don't you understand? I have an orchard in my grounds with many orange trees. Why not visit me later and I will show you quite an excellent trick. Come tonight!"

Don Fernán bowed his head and went on his way.

He whistled a soft tune composed long ago by Bertran de Born, one of the greatest minstrels of any age.

He climbed the stairs to the battlements, paced the full length of them, up the gradient and down again; then back. At the highest point he paused to string his bow and nock an arrow. Then he leaned over and scanned the blue sky. There was a stork: not heading south to Granada, but northwest, to Castile or perhaps even Galicia.

Lands of other true believers. Friends.

Don Fernán looked around, saw that nobody had noticed.

And he shot the arrow anyway!

The arrow grazed the stork and did not bring it down; but it dropped in fright the bundle it was carrying in its beak. Don Fernán was amazed! Not for one moment had he believed his own lie to Baron Antonio. He hurried down the steps, through the gate and out onto the scrub. In anticipation of finding the mangled body of an unborn child, he perspired and cursed and groaned; but that wasn't what it was.

It was a wooden cup, undamaged by the fall.

What was a stork doing with such an object? Don Fernán deduced that the wisest course of action was to keep it for himself and mention nothing of how he had come to acquire it.

And so he carried it home in his quiver.

His mother was trying to open a new bottle of wine. "Medicine!" she snapped at him, almost defensively, and he was forced to agree with that definition of the rich red liquid.

Doña Isabella belched in his face and he recoiled at the pungency of the emitted fumes as he helped her open the bottle properly. Poor soul! She must be suffering from a most vicious malady if even six bottles a day wasn't sufficient to cure it. Probably the dose should be increased to eight. And yet the Baron's invitation—

Don Fernán went to visit him shortly after sunset. Baron Antonio was delighted to receive his guest. He gave the knight a tour of his house and took him to see his orange trees, picking a dozen of the largest fruits and throwing them across to Don Fernán.

"You expect me to learn juggling, my lord?"

Baron Antonio laughed and said, "In my opinion, instead of allowing your mother to serve herself with medicine, you should prepare it for her with your own hands. What better example of filial loyalty can there be? But be sure to squeeze these fruits first and mix the wine with the juice in adjusted proportions every time."

"Orange juice and wine blended together!"

"Yes, yes, dear boy; don't look so disgusted until you have tried it! I'm proud to have invented a new beverage, which I call *sangria* because of its resemblance to blood. I am sure it will catch on eventually! But this is the important point. Are you listening? The first time you serve it to Doña Isabella, there must be far more wine than juice. Very slowly increase the ratio of juice to wine. Before the arrival of winter you should have only a small amount of wine in the brew."

Don Fernán scratched his head. "What will that achieve?"

Baron Antonio licked his lips and said, "Done carefully, it may result in your mother's complete recovery."

Don Fernán nodded. If his mother got better, he would be free to run away to the wars raging in the east.

The Baron added, "I will call a slave to pick all the other oranges and put them in a sack for you. I will give you enough to last two months. At the end of that time, more will ripen."

Don Fernán thanked him and returned home.

Over the following days and weeks, the impetuous knight followed the instructions he had been given. He proceeded to adulterate the wine, but he did it by such small degrees that his mother didn't seem to notice; or if she did notice, then she didn't care sufficiently to object. He served it to her promptly whenever she called him.

After the space of two months, Baron Antonio paid a visit, leaving his slaves and litter outside in the street. The youthful knight showed him to where his mother sat, still in her chair, raising a full cup of sangria to her lips; and yes, her health had improved.

But the Baron choked and clutched his throat.

"That cup! That cup!" he wailed.

"Merely a wooden drinking vessel," said Don Fernán.

"No, no! It's the Grail itself!"

"How is that possible? The Grail is in Italy—"

"The Grail is in so many places, my boy, so many places. Nevertheless *that* cup is the genuine article. I have studied the subject and I know. How did you come upon it? How?"

"A stork dropped it," muttered Don Fernán.

"Did you shoot the bird?"

"At it, yes; but my arrow missed."

The Baron eyes widened. "And it was taking it south to Granada? You only fire at storks flying in that direction, you said! So why was the Grail being delivered to our enemies, to unbelievers? I must consult the Church for moral guidance on this matter."

"Maybe the stork stole it from somewhere?"

"No, no! Nothing so significant ever happens by accident! The year is 1313. Maybe that has something to do with it? Thirteen guests at the Last Supper? Thirteen thirteen: something of deep numerological significance no doubt! One Grail for us; one for them! Armageddon and the end of all Time. Maybe even two Gods—"

Don Fernán shuffled his feet nervously.

"We have it now," he said.

The Baron rushed to the side of Doña Isabella, snatched the cup out of her hand and lifted it to his nose.

He sniffed and his face contorted in shame.

There is no overriding reason why orange juice shouldn't be drunk out of the Holy Grail. There was never an edict forbidding it. No parable, legend or rule has ever warned of the dangers of doing so. There is no disrespect inherent in the action, none at all.

No one who later learned details of this case, which includes you right now, has ever had an argument why it's wrong to do so. But it still doesn't *seem* right. Fine to sip and swallow wine from the cup; that's obvious. But not orange juice, not even when mixed with wine. Sangria in the Sangraal feels like a very arcane blasphemy.

To ensure that nothing like this could happen again, the Baron ordered the chopping down of every orange tree in Albarracín, including his own. And nobody was allowed to plant an orange pip, a custom that continues, though everybody has forgotten why it occurs. Try ordering sangria in the cafés of that town; you won't get it.

The Man Toucan

God was peering over the edge of Heaven and enjoying himself by trying to see shapes in the clouds above Spain. "That one looks like a ghost and this other like a dragon!" he guffawed.

As these capricious argosies of moisture swirled and reformed, chance on its own made it inevitable that some would assume outlines that might seem significant, ominous or profound.

"Hey, that Cirrocumulus lacunosus undulatus looks like an angel. Wait a moment – it *is* an angel! It must be returning from a mission on Earth or maybe it is trying out new wings."

God wiped tears of mirth from his cheeks.

"This is such fun! I'm glad I invented clouds… Now *that* one is a dead ringer for The Devil. What a lark!

"And that one looks like a lark. What a wheeze!"

As the clouds parted and dispersed, he found himself gazing down into a landscape that didn't look familiar at all. He pulled his beard, combing it with his fingers, and frowned deeply.

"I don't recall ever seeing that region of Spain before! I thought I knew the entire country very well; but clearly I have overlooked one corner. It's in the far south of Aragon too, which makes it even more surprising. Why have I forgotten about this realm?"

He studied it more closely and saw a small city built of red stones with an ancient wall that crawled up a hill and down again: inside the wall was a castle, cathedral and tangle of narrow streets that undulated between tall houses and converged on a humble *plaza*. Everything about it seemed too quaint to be true. God was intrigued.

"I don't even recall the name of that place down there! It reminds me a little of Alpuente, but it's even more picturesque. I suppose I ought to pay a visit in person, as I sometimes do."

The truth is that God rarely visited the surface of Earth; there were too many other planets in the universe to attend to. But occasionally he put on typical human garb and took the plunge; and when he did so, Spain was a favoured destination. He changed his clothes quickly, slipped his feet into sandals and jumped over the side.

Down through outer space he plummeted.

Galaxies brushed his elbows and knees, and some of the stars in them were knocked out of alignment and banged into others, so he straightened his legs and kept his arms at his sides and shot like a vertical comet right into the thick cream of the Milky Way.

He grew constantly smaller as he fell, contracting evenly. Soon he was no bigger than the largest black hole.

Heaven would continue to work in his absence. The cosmos was like a vast clock and only needed winding once an aeon. Tiny adjustments were constantly needed to stop evolution deviating from the plan, but inorganic processes could look after themselves.

At last, after an entire hour of motion, shrinking all the time, he passed through the atmosphere of Earth and landed on solid ground, still glowing white hot from the friction, absorbing the impact by rolling over and over in the stunted rosemary bushes, setting some on fire but stamping out the little blazes with his oversized sandals.

His aim had been pretty good, but not perfect.

The main road to the mysterious city lay a dozen strides to his left. As he continued to cool, he set off over the rocky ground. His foot knocked a stone that chimed; no, it wasn't a stone.

A bottle, ancient and dusty and long forgotten.

He picked it up, peered intently.

Then he shook it and held it against his ear.

"What do we have here? It looks very old and I suspect it was dropped many decades ago or more; perhaps even whole centuries have rolled past since its owner lost it. Does it contain wine? I doubt it. Let me tug out the cork and gingerly sniff the contents!"

But before he could lift the vessel to his nostrils, a green mist billowed out of the neck of the bottle and congealed into the form of a fat man with an enormous turban on his head. This peculiar figure bowed very low and intoned deeply, "Your wish is my—"

God was impressed. "A cloud imprisoned in a bottle! And it has taken on the shape of a genie! It's incredible. Are you the cheeky Cirrocumulus lacunosus undulatus I noticed earlier?"

"No, indeed; I'm a genuine genie at your command."

God pulled his beard. "A genie in Spain? Are you sure? I thought your kind were confined to eastern parts."

The genie smiled graciously, bowed again and replied, "Ah, but until recently, Spain *was* part of the East. The date is only 1499 and so it has been a mere seven years since the last Muslim kingdom was overthrown, and there still exist many Arabs in the Alpujarras hills south of Granada and they have independence down there even now; but of course Aragon has been Christian for three centuries."

"I'm delighted with your grasp of history!"

The genie clasped his hands together and nodded, the green diadem on his green turban flashing greenly. "The *reconquista* is of vital interest to all followers of the three main faiths."

God conceded this point. "I suppose it is. But tell me what is the name of that lovely rose-tinted little city? I appear to have forgotten everything about it, which is an unusual circumstance for sure; it instils in me a dark suspicion there might be other corners of this planet that have escaped my attention of late. And if there are, it would explain a lot about why people have started doubting my existence."

"That is Albarracín," replied the genie.

"Hmm, I can't honestly say the name is familiar, but it has a nice ring to it. Surely nothing happens there?"

"An obscure city, true enough. It was an independent emirate for one century; a sovereign Christian kingdom for another; now it is merely part of the greater Castilian overlordship that has united the entire country. As for myself, I was dropped by an alchemist fleeing the overthrow of the *taifa* of the Banu Razin dynasty by the Almoravids of Morocco in 1104. A vigorous race, the Almoravids, and no one could oppose them. I still recall with a shudder the soldiers marching with their banners. Did you know that the flag of Morocco back then was a perfect chessboard with red and white squares? Often the troops on campaign spread them on the ground and played bouts while resting."

"You've been stuck in this bottle all that time?"

"Yes, but there's no oddness to it. The alchemist saw that the road was blocked by oncoming horsemen, so he scurried away over the scrub and I slipped out of his pocket just a few strides from the road; very few people ever leave the roads in these parts, so I was never found until now. I have been waiting for rescue very patiently."

"In that case I'm glad I stumbled over you," said God.

The genie answered, "In accordance with the strict laws of my kind, I must now grant you three wishes."

God was amused. "Wishes? For me!"

"The laws of my kind make no distinction between mortals and higher entities. Whoever liberates me earns three wishes, simple as that. It's not compulsory to use them, however."

God frowned deeply. His first impulse was to decline politely, for not since the first moment of creation had he ever utilised a power other than his own to achieve his aims; but with just a little more thought he decided there could no harm in making use of the genie's offer. Even deities want certain things; that's no dishonour.

He cleared his throat and said, "Very well, but I only require one wish. Save the other two for some other fortunate passerby, for I'm not greedy. As for my single wish, I want to be relieved of responsibility. It's the only thing I desire, but I *do* yearn for it!"

Green eyes blinked. "Responsibility for what?"

God made an expansive gesture with both hands that encompassed the landscape, the sky and the eternal void beyond. "The universe, the whole picture, reality, creation itself, *everything*. I am so tired of it. I'm weary of the enormous responsibility. I've had enough. I no longer want to be held to account for the cosmos. I realise the buck needs to stop somewhere but I don't want it to be *me* any longer."

The genie bowed low again. "I comprehend."

"Can you do it? Shift blame from me to someone else? The persistence of existence is my work alone, I'll never deny that, but the responsibility's a heavy burden I could do without."

The genie answered, "Yes, it's a feasible wish, but who should take the responsibility for you? Do you have a particular individual in mind? One of your heretical enemies, perhaps?"

God shook his head. "No, no, I'm not that vindictive! To make it fair, I think it should be the next random person who comes along and discovers your bottle. That's a neat solution."

The genie bowed so low his turban stirred dust.

"At your command. I must point out, however, that it may be a century or more before anyone else comes this way again. I base this estimate on experience. Carry my bottle nearer the road and you won't have so long to wait before your wish is discharged."

God agreed this was a fine idea and stooped to pick up the bottle while the genie spiralled back down the neck. Striding over the scrub, God set down the vessel on the edge of the road; then bade the genie farewell and set off in the direction of Albarracín.

The genie waited in the depths of the bottle. God hadn't put the cork back in, so technically he was free to go, but his sense of propriety kept him a voluntary captive; he was determined to divest himself of all three wishes before enjoying his freedom properly.

A few days passed. At last a figure was seen approaching slowly from the city. It was a man and he walked like one who has gone for a stroll to clear a fuddled mind, not because he has anywhere in particular he wants to be, sighing constantly as he trudged.

The genie recognised his attire as that of a bishop.

He whistled softly through his green lips to subtly attract the attention of the new arrival and the bishop stopped in his tracks, squinted at the road and observed the bottle gleaming in the sunlight. He approached, seized it and examined it with a dark brown eye.

"Some sort of elemental spirit trapped within!"

The genie emerged, congealed itself and bowed. "I wasn't trapped, but I have two wishes to offer you anyway. Don't ask me why there isn't three available; it just happened that way."

The bishop sat down on the verge and said, "Two wishes are plenty for any man or woman who isn't a fool."

"I take it you don't put yourself in that category?"

"That's not really for me to judge. Perhaps I am a fool after all; I am Juan Marrades, bishop of Segorbe and Albarracín, and I succeeded the renowned Bartolomé Martí only last year. I don't think my sinecure will last much longer. I haven't done well."

"There have been complaints about your behaviour?"

"No, nothing like that. It's a political question only. There are people pulling strings in hidden places; I have my allies but my enemies are no less cunning or rancorous than we are. The problem is that I have plenty of responsibility and a certain amount of power; but the responsibility is far greater than the power. Imbalance."

"That word is a synonym for trouble," said the genie.

The bishop nodded. "Well put!"

"Do you care to employ your two wishes now?"

The bishop adjusted his mitre and said, "I'll take one. Keep the other for the next person who wanders this way. This is what I want: to have the *exact* amount of power that is commensurate with my responsibility, no more, no less. Give me that precise amount of power and I'll ask no more for the remainder of my life."

The genie felt a sudden chill envelop his frame. "You are wishing for parity between the power available to you and the responsibility you are lumbered with? Are you quite sure?"

The bishop nodded. "Yes, yes. Get on with it!"

The genie swallowed with difficulty but obeyed the laws of his kind without protest. When the wish was granted, he vanished back inside the bottle while the bishop stood and stretched himself, flexing muscles that felt infinitely stronger than before.

"I came out for a simple walk, for an hour of peace before returning to the fray of church politics, and it was clearly the best decision I've made for a long time. I feel invigorated!"

The genie said nothing and the bishop soon found that the novelty of stretching his limbs wore off. He began walking back to Albarracín, but with a powerful spring in his step.

*

The genie didn't have long to wait to meet the next traveller. A few hours later, another figure came hurrying up the road. The sun was setting and it seemed the stranger was wearing clothes dyed in sunset juice that would darken with dusk, but they remained scarlet. Clearly he was an alchemist or philosopher of some new variety.

He noticed the bottle from the corner of his eye.

"A genie! How remarkable!"

"Your wish is my command. Only one wish, though…"

"Half a wish would be enough for me at present! I am Oroondates de Gris. That's not my real name, but I'm an immigrant from Portugal and a student, or I might say master, of the art of measuring abstract things; our discipline doesn't have official papal approval yet, so it's safer to employ pseudonyms. None of this is relevant, so I'll reveal that my own speciality is the measuring of vibrations on the spiritual plane and my apparatus has detected a most peculiar flux of energies. The readings are unmistakable. There are now *two* Gods at large in the universe. Two Gods! I can't guess where the other one came from!"

"Does this situation necessarily spell disaster?"

"Probably. One God has infinite power but no responsibility; the other has infinite responsibility and the power to go with it. They aren't exactly matched, but I can't for the life of me guess who is stronger. It's curious and very frightening. Physically, the battlements and towers of the city are as steady as before, but in spiritual terms they are being pulled apart by opposing webs of omnipotence!"

"I share your dismay at this news," said the genie.

Oroondates gasped, "Let me use that single wish immediately! I don't want to be a man if the two Gods decide to come to blows. Man is made in the divine image, after all, and has free will and conscience, and so will be forced to choose sides; I'd rather be an innocent animal, something that can't ever be asked to commit itself."

"Ah yes, I understand. A simple lowly beast such as a weasel or pig? I can do that for you easily enough—"

"Halt! I don't want to be *common*. I want to be striking, a candidate for celebrity, just in case the two Gods don't actually start fighting. Just over six years ago, a new continent was discovered in the west, a territory full of strange new mammals and colourful birds. I want to be a toucan, a bird that is perfectly adapted to its milieu despite its mildly absurd appearance. Turn me into a toucan without delay!"

The genie didn't need to know what a toucan looked like to fulfill this request; a wish contains its own specifications. But he regarded the bright bird with admiration and asked, "Where will you go now? South! A wise choice of direction!" He rubbed his green chin and added, "Will you take me along if I roll myself into a nut?"

The bird nodded; the genie compressed himself. The bird grasped him in its beak, taking care not to swallow him, flapped its wings and soared into the sky, a dazzling intermittent flash of colour. At this spectacle, the younger clouds above were amazed.

"Look at the size of its nose!"

That's how the first toucan came to Spain.

But originally it was a man.

Latitude, Longitude and Plenitude

Year of Our Lord, 1687.

To Your Grace, the wise and superlative Miguel Jerónimo Fuenbuena, Bishop of Albarracín, I offer the humble greetings of an Inspector of Sea Walls in the proximity of Valencia.

My name is Carlos Delgado and I am an old man.

Whether by providential design or the whims of chance, I recently had the once in a lifetime experience of fishing out from the ocean's bosom a murky green glass bottle containing a message. Both are even older than I am; the message is written on a type of parchment that went out of vogue near the end of the previous century.

The message appears to be addressed to your predecessor, Bernardino Gómes Miedes, who was Bishop of Albarracín exactly one hundred years ago. I say 'appears' because the beginning of the message has been ruined by a small leak; the bottle was not hermetically sealed. Nonetheless a date can be deduced from the actual text.

I enclose not only the original parchment with this present letter but an accurate transcription of the same, for the handwriting of the author is not of the greatest clarity. His name was Gabriel Caballero and he was native to your city; this is why I now consider it my duty to forward his message and also the bottle itself to you. I have confidence that you will find what is written to be of surpassing interest.

The tale that Gabriel Caballero tells in this parchment solves a mystery that has long troubled my family: my father was the obscure conquistador Lucas Agustín Delgado, who sought to match the exploits of Pizarro and others of that ilk, but who found the chronicles of his campaigns censored inexplicably by the unjust authorities.

As expected, I seek to restore my sire's good reputation and so will be grateful for any help Your Grace may see fit to extend to me. At the end of the transcribed parchment message, I attach the relevant page from my father's personal logbook; both screeds complement each other. I remain your servant, in all good faith. Amen.

THE TESTAMENT OF THE CASTAWAY

...and the final waves did wash overboard all my companions. Now was I alone on the ship; and falling to my knees I prayed, blasphemously, to the sea itself to deliver me from harm. And lo! was my plea answered, for the clouds did suddenly part; and there before me, impaled on sunbeams like a boar riddled with spears, was a tropic island! At once a shivering seized hold of me, for I had shown grave weakness by soliciting the deeps, and I wondered whose debt was I in? And I was reminded of the horrid fate of those who make pacts with demons and end up in the hands of the blessed and holy but unappealing Inquisition.

There and then, I vowed to cleanse and purify my eternal soul through my own efforts before anyone else sought to do it; for the Inquisition has an attitude to such matters that I like not. Yet even this dreadful question was of less immediate importance than the preservation of my body in the wild waters of the churned sea. The tormented galleon had lodged upon a reef and the currents were tearing her apart. Unable to launch a longboat on my own, I had no choice but to fling myself into the briny embrace of the angry ocean. Despite my upbringing in the highlands, I am a swimmer of considerable stamina and strength.

At last I hauled myself onto a shore of white sand, my knees bleeding from contact with the coral, my lungs rasping unpleasantly; but although I had no supplies or victuals of any kind, not even a knife or husk of bread,

I was alive and grateful enough for the fact. I lay panting on the beach for more than an hour, while the rain and wind lessened its force and the tiny parting in the clouds widened to show the beautiful blue of the empyrean, and soon I was lapped dry by the tongue of the sun; and if I felt not joy in the caress, then for certain I was soothed and comforted. Yet still did I not stir, but remained prone on my back.

The fleeing clouds were formless, unlike those of my childhood town, isolated but noble Albarracín, forgotten up in the mountains, where every vapour was an actor with a shape not its own. I thought of that place and of Spain in general, readying for war with England, building an armada to sail against the heretic queen in her northern cesspit, and I could not envy too much those who were still there. I did not love war myself, and cared not to absorb the blow of a cannonball in the service of any cause, though let it be noted carefully that I was willing to join our armada for reasons of duty, and was prevented only by fate.

At last I regained sufficient strength and sense to stand and survey my surroundings. It was an island such as many others off the coast of Africa and I wondered if it was a Portuguese possession. If so, I could expect no mercy from our rivals in conquest; then I remembered that Portugal was a vassal of Spain and had been for a full seven years. You ask, how could I have forgotten a fact so significant? I reply that it was clearly a symptom of a disordered set of senses: the storm and mental shock of my condition had softened the pulpy matter inside my skull. I was a temporary fool and needed food and spiced wine to recover.

I walked along the shore, calling out, hoping to attract the attention of any inhabitants, but my cries were greeted with silence. Then I noticed a face among the palms; it was a man's and did not seem eager to eat me. I had heard stories about cannibals on the mainland, yet it was too late for such apprehensions. I smiled and made encouraging noises at my watcher and his head vanished, only to return with two others; finally they braved themselves to approach. Naked they were, and innocent as babes, holding spears tipped not with metal but stone. I continued to croon and cluck my tongue until they stood right before me.

They said nothing, nor did they prostrate themselves, and acutely did I become aware that I was no god to them, nothing special at all, merely an object thrown up by the waves, of passing interest and not valuable in any practical way. I know that maroons do become kings of tribes as often as they are turned into stew, but evidently neither fate was to be mine. First I pointed at myself and said the name, "Gabriel" as clearly as possible. This seemed to me a logical first step in the teaching of my language, but even this simple action was misinterpreted. I later learned that they had thought I was referring to the torn short I wore.

Thirst and hunger drove me to great efforts. I pointed at various items in the vicinity, at the trees, the coconuts hanging from them; the sea, sand and waves; the sky and sun; speaking the word for each precisely, but the sun alone produced a reaction. They began giggling and shaking, though when I looked again I saw no reason for their mirth: the sun was burning as usual in its appointed place. In time I discovered that sunbeams were a kind of tickle on their faces; I still do not know why this should be so. At last they grew bored with my demonstration and simply wandered away. I was amazed at their calm indifference.

Fearful to be left alone again, I followed them at a distance with gentle footfalls, but even when a shell crunched loudly under my boot these men did not deign to turn around. They appeared to have lost interest in me, as if I was a fashion that had gone out of date. I did well to tell myself that a question of latitude and longitude is the crucial point of any philosophical debate on customs and morals. What is wrong on one side of a mountain range can be right on the other; the same truth applies to islands and seas. In Albarracín we deem it most offensive to ignore strangers, but the same behaviour here might be good manners.

I followed them for more than an hour through tangled steamy jungle, staining my clothes with sap from unknown plants, until at last we burst into a large clearing. This was the exact centre of the island, and here the savages had constructed their village. Women and children were waiting to greet the men, but they paid me no heed. I was free to study the village in peace. What intrigued me most were the huts, which far from showing the roundness of most African dwellings were rectangular, more like the tall houses of my beloved Spain. They had been raised close together and many even helped to prop each other up.

Wandering up the primitive streets I expected to be apprehended and taken prisoner, but the inhabitants continued to treat me as irrelevant. No more unsettling reaction can be imagined. I was obviously a newcomer of outlandish appearance, worthy of comment and action, yet I may as well have been a chicken flapping in the dust, or a cat padding from threshold to threshold in search of edible morsels. "Gabriel!" I said to myself with a sour smile, "What topsy-turvy world have you entered? I am the civilised man and they the brutes; yet I now feel like the lowest of island denizens and unworthy of any respect at all…"

I sat on a tree stump and waited. Nothing.

"For the love of God!" I shouted.

Still there was no response from anyone. Had I turned invisible? What sin had I committed to be condemned to this miserable situation! I might as well confess that I blasphemed and ranted, jumping up and waving my arms to attract attention. At last I was forced to seize a woman around the waist and drag her close to me; then I covered her neck in hot kisses. She twisted and scowled with annoyance rather than true fear. Suddenly I felt a pinprick in my own neck. A blowpipe dart was lodged there. Down into the hot dust I sank, my vision rotating as if my eyes were wheels, and the sleep that overcame me was profound.

Hours of dreamless sleep passed in a blink.

I woke and nothing had changed. Still was I prone in the middle of the dirty street in a hidden village of square huts and nobody cared when I sat erect and struggled to my feet. I understood that if I molested any woman again, or any man, I would receive another forced sleep, then a third, and so on until the basic lesson was learned. I was a keen pupil and needed no second demonstration of the power of the herbal ointment with which the dart were smeared. I would be left to my own devices and tolerated, free to come and go as I pleased; but any action that disturbed community life would be firmly, implacably dealt with.

This existence was something I had scant appetite for. I stumbled back into the trees and when dusk overtook me there, I spent an uncomfortable night in the wide branches of a baobab, listening out for wild animals but hearing none. The following morning I returned to the coast, to the site of my original beaching; and there, to my glee, I discovered that many items from the wrecked galleon had been carried ashore by the currents. Chests full of fabrics, casks of rum and wine, sealed boxes containing parchment and bottles of ink, others packed with biscuits; all these were mine by law and necessity, and I accepted them gladly.

At first I supposed I might inaugurate a culture on the coast that neatly would contrast with the inland culture of the indigenous inhabitants. They were slaves to nature's laws, lacking interior illumination, intoxicants and silken breeches, while I would live almost in a European style; but foolish indeed was this dream, for I was but one solitary man. My efforts to build a reliable shelter, to keep livestock and grow crops were doomed from the start. I was never so dedicated or skilled as I liked to believe; and I lacked the appropriate tools. As the weeks passed, a return to the village became a more and more appealing proposition.

And that is precisely what I did. I went back.

Still did everyone there ignore me. Yet this time the final outcome was different, thanks to providence or luck.

Some men were having difficulties starting a fire. It had rained during the night and the wood and leaves were damp. I had a scroll of parchment with me, for I had planned to try to impress them into acknowledging my existence by teaching them arithmetic, a vain hope indeed. Now I realised that an alternative use for the blank page might be more effective. Around the firepit was an empty space and I squatted there, turning the parchment with a few twists into a taper. Flint and steel from my pocket made sparks and those sparks conjured flames in the taper hot enough to glow, crackle and then fully bloom the sodden sticks.

The result of this was a few appreciative murmurs.

I moved into the village at once.

Yet I had only been accepted to the slightest degree and the occasional smile was the most intense form of interaction I ever had during my stay. I had to forage for my own food and build my own hut without help from any of my neighbours; but I was allowed to light the communal fire every evening; and this duty afforded me a genuine pleasure. I felt more secure among these people than on my own on the beach: snakes and other wild animals, if indeed there were any, kept away from the clearing. True, the chances of being rescued were lessened, but so too the risks of falling into the vicious hands of Barbary corsairs.

The main problem I had was to adjust my own values to those of these people. They had little concept of the sanctity of personal property. Many of my possessions were pilfered within weeks; even sheets of parchment were taken, for the natives held its properties as tinder in high regard, and the hours I spent protesting at this presumption were wasted. Soon almost half my stock had vanished and I grew agitated. I had planned to write an account of my adventures on the island, so that if I died before rescue my story would endure and perhaps even reach my countrymen, letting them know what had befallen their brother.

But it quickly became apparent that my writings were not safe. Even a page covered in the finest handwriting had no greater value to the natives than a blank sheet; they stole it from my hut and burned it, and so phrases of ingenuity and elegance were utilised to roast yams and cassava. Hiding my work in hollow trees did not work, for they rotted there or turned vile and mushy with fungus. I realised that my only option was to consign my writings to the waves in an empty bottle. The document I set adrift in that manner is the one you are presently reading; and if you are not reading it, then perhaps it is still at sea, unfound.

Yet the chances of it arriving on any shore are very slim. A whale may swallow the bottle, or it may shatter on rocks or drift on random currents to the end of time. Even after I seal the bottle and throw it into the waves, I will be desirous of leaving a record for those later explorers who might discover this village in this clearing in the centre of this island. Yes, I will want them to know that I, Gabriel Caballero of Albarracín, was here first, during the Golden Age of Spain, when our ships braved the waters of the furthest corners of the ill-adjusted globe. But how may I accomplish this? How to ensure a *permanent* message?

To leave a written record in the care of my neighbours is impracticable for the reasons I have given; the building of a monument in stone is also out of the question, for there is no workable stone on the island. To scribe my tale not in ink but in the blood of future generations, in other words to beget so many children that explorers who encounter my descendants will guess the origin of their fair complexions, is another frustrated option, for the native women do not allow me near them but regard me as ugly in the extreme; and to force myself upon them like a slaver would result in more drugged darts. What solution is there?

And one detail I have not yet mentioned…

It is important that this message is not merely a general statement that once a white castaway dwelled here, but that he was so-and-so from such-and-such a place. I seek precision…

Yes, that makes the task harder. And so?

I believe I have found an answer. I believe that even if this message in a bottle is never found, future explorers who land on the island, explore it carefully and see what I have done, will be able to work out my story and know truly that it is Gabriel Caballero's. This is what I did. I built myself a second hut. I constructed it next to my first. When it was ready I started on a third, and so on. Each hut was slightly different from its neighbour; I was very exact in proportions, if not dimensions. The natives offered only the assistance of their stares and laughter, but it was enough to encourage me, for it meant they were *interested*.

My memory is better than that of many men.

I recalled the exact layout of the streets and alleys, the central *plaza*; I could not accurately imitate the walls, but I used the edge of the clearing as a substitute. Finally I had it! After years of toil I had made a permanent message, with nothing there for the natives to steal; or rather, its theft, the abandonment of their own huts to move into mine, was a guarantee of its preservation and upkeep. I had replicated my childhood home, populated it with brave citizens, and thus my main message had been written. As for *this* message, the one you are reading: it is of lesser consequence. All the same, I will now cast it into the waves.

FROM THE LOG OF LUCAS AGUSTÍN DELGADO

The island was inhabited and the savages proved no match for our guns and swords. We slaughtered about half of them in the jungle itself; then we followed the survivors back to their village. Truly a sight of wonder awaited us there! Some of us fell on our knees and begged forgiveness from the Almighty, for clearly these savages were civilised men and did not deserve the same treatment as that given to ignorant idolaters. And clearly do I remember the words of one soldier who said, "Let us kill no more of them, but leave them in peace and return to our own lands," and another soldier went even further and added, "And let us erase from our sea-charts the position of this island."

Plenitude comes in many forms, and I have beheld it in gold, jewels, fine horses, ivory, pearls and women; but this was a plenitude of wonder, for the wisdom of our institutions proclaims that uncivilised men cannot build cities of their own, especially not cities as fine and delightful to the eye as this one. I understood the requests of my men. I knew deep in my heart that there was a mystery here to be solved, but an ancient hatred in my soul frothed up and drowned my reason; and I charged headlong into the first house and cut the walls to pieces with my sword. Compelled to follow where I led, to mimic my actions, my soldiers chopped up houses of their own; and soon all was ruined.

I have destroyed the mystery and for this I will surely be criticised. I accept the inevitability of the outcome with a head held high with pride. Since I was a boy, sitting on the knee of my grandfather on the quayside of Valencia, I have been told tales of my valiant ancestor, Louis the Wolf, and how he was tortured in the dungeons of Albarracín. There is unity in Spain now; how can I take revenge against that city? I would be a traitor to my king and country. So I have kept my passions in check. Now I ask for understanding, not forgiveness. When I sail down the coast of Africa to an uncharted isle and find there a perfect replica of the city that once humiliated my great-great-great-great-great-great-great-great grandfather how can I not revenge myself upon it?

The Kind Generosity of Theophrastus Tautology

It was the weirdest house in Albarracín.

Not only was it misshapen, but it was constructed from odd materials, namely bricks of almost opaque glass that caught the heavy beams of the rising sun and refracted them at unexpected angles through the walls into the interior rooms. Turquoise glass.

Certainly no habitation for ordinary men!

Which is why two inquisitors found themselves approaching the front door, which fortunately was made of honest fig wood; one of them with a professional frown, the other with a thick iron rod that might be used as a portable knocker on suspicious portals.

"Surely he is at home; note how the chimney smokes?"

The inquisitor with the metal bar sighed and stroked his pointed beard with his free hand. "Yes, Ignacio, but watch how the smoke pours *into* the chimney as if sucked by a giant mouth. This fireplace works in reverse. I have never heard tell of such a thing!"

Ignacio crossed himself. "Are we too late?"

The other inquisitor shook his head. "What choice did we have? These are dark times and the body we represent no longer commands respect or fear; the intellectuals laugh at us, even the peasants mock. Soon we might have no power at all. The Bishop did everything to discourage us; I don't think he even believes in the Devil."

Ignacio spat on the ground. "That for Joaquín González de Terán, foul traitor to the cause of holiness!"

"Be less vocal in your condemnations, brother."

"Forgive me, Atanasio."

The year was 1808 and the superstitions of the past were fading across Europe, even in Spain, partly because of Napoleon and his campaigns. To the conservative minds of these inquisitors, the dominance of reason over faith was a cataclysm without precedent. Yet they hadn't abandoned hope entirely; they still plied their trade.

Atanasio raised his iron and pounded on the door.

Then he lowered it and waited.

There came a sound of creaking that grew louder; then the sliding of a bolt and the door opened. A figure stood grinning at them in the doorway, thin and gangly, his limbs and neck as loose as those of a puppet, yet with a curious awkwardness about them; when he moved any part of himself to a new position, the creak sounded.

He blinked his protesting eyelids. "Yes?"

Ignacio moved forward with the scroll of disdain, already unrolled and fully extended before him as he read it aloud. "Señor Tautology, son of an unknown father and mother, origin of both unknown, with other pertinent details of your life equally unknown, you stand accused of sorcery, to wit dabbling with spells, devils or spirits to the detriment of public order and the utter peril of your eternal soul..."

"Sorcery." Atanasio repeated that one word with a thin smile, a malign grin, the smirk of a fanatic. The lean figure shrugged audibly, held out his empty hands and said with a sigh:

"I won't deny it. You have caught me at last!"

Atanasio felt his jaw slacken.

Ignacio raised an eyebrow. "You openly admit the charge is true? But that's what the torture is for: to make you confess your crimes! What's the point of pain if you admit it now?"

"You aren't playing the game," hissed Atanasio.

"I'm guilty," said Theophrastus.

The inquisitors were bewildered...

"Come with us; that is an order. By the authority of the Inquisition! To our Toledo dungeons we will take you," intoned Ignacio, "along the bank of the River Tajo, a long journey!"

"We will ride; you must walk," sniffed Atanasio.

Theophrastus pondered this.

"Come inside first," he finally said.

Ignacio and Atanasio exchanged glances and the latter pointed his iron rod at the face of the self-defined sorcerer. "It has never been customary for agents of the Inquisition to accept the hospitality of their enemies! We are unkind to our prisoners, we don't cosset them, and we scarcely expect them to treat us with kindness in return. Or are you planning a trick? Both of us are armed with prayers to counter black magic! In the pocket of my robe is a finger bone of St. Murk."

Theophrastus nodded. "Then you have nothing to fear."

Atanasio said, "That's true."

"So come inside for just a few minutes."

"But why *should* we?"

Theophrastus rubbed his lantern jaw; it gave off no light, but there was a greenish tinge to it, almost as if it had once been phosphorescent but the glow had worn off over long ages. "Time is running out for all, for you no less than me, as I'm sure you are aware. Suppose I accompany you now to the dungeons of Toledo, a walk of two weeks? How many extra weeks of obtaining witnesses and preparing paperwork will be necessary before the case is won and you can kill me?"

"Our protocols are meticulous, of course!"

"You have no hard evidence against me; only my word. That means a trial to prove I am not a madman. By the time you are given the go ahead for an *auto-da-fé*, a public garrotting or burning, the French will already have won the war and the Inquisition will be dissolved. All your strivings will be in vain, utterly wasted. But if you come inside now and permit me to give you a quick tour of my house, you will emerge with real evidence of my vile dealings with sorcery."

Without waiting for a response, he turned on his heel and creaked back into the depths of his glass abode.

"I am disconcerted," muttered Ignacio. "His perverse generosity in this matter is unprecedented in history—"

Atanasio gripped his iron like a club. "Don't be fooled, brother! This is simply a ruse to distract us and weaken our resolve! Let us venture inside anyway and do our best to turn his cunning against him! Señor Tautology will rue the day he jested with us!"

They stepped through the open door.

Without thinking, Ignacio closed it behind him. Later he fretted at not having left it open, for an easier exit, but he forgave himself for what was simply a reflex. He followed Atanasio. The passage was straight, narrow, eerie, but not too long. Theophrastus Tautology was waiting patiently at the end, where it opened out into a room, a chamber lined with odd glass cases that were actually huge bottles.

From the top of each bottle twisted a hollow glass tube; these tubes all joined up together and formed a thicker tube, and this wider conduit went through a hole in the wall into an adjacent room. Every bottle contained a shape, and the shapes were alarming.

"Don't be apprehensive," soothed Theophrastus.

"What are they?" cried Atanasio.

Theophrastus explained as gently as a museum curator, "As a sorcerer I'm capable of doing many fantastic things; summoning up the long-dead is my finest trick. Before you are many different personages from sundry ages in Albarracín's amazing history!"

Ignacio and Atanasio peered at the nearest bottle.

"Who is *he*?" asked the former.

Theophrastus looked over the inquisitor's shoulder. "Ah, that is one of the ambassadors of 'Abd Allah the First, emir of the *taifa* of Alpuente, the favoured neighbour of our own city when Albarracín was also ruled by a Moorish kinglet. He is from the early Eleventh Century, this fellow, and I don't think he's unhappy behind glass."

"May we converse with him?" demanded Atanasio.

The sorcerer shook his head doubtfully. "Only if you speak Arabic or Mozarabic. Do you? I didn't think so."

Ignacio said, "And who is that next to him?"

"An English knight," answered Theophrastus, "who arrived in the city because he wanted more glory than might be found at home. He died in a fall. He fell for a woman, fatally—"

"I like this not," shuddered Atanasio.

"He speaks not only English, but Arabic and Mozarabic. And Hebrew too. He was a very able student."

"Why learn infidel tongues?" spat Ignacio.

"Back then," continued the sorcerer, "the west *was* the east. Now, alas, it seems the east is trying too hard to become the west. But let's pass on to the third bottle. What do you think of this mighty warrior? Louis the Wolf is how he was known: a mercenary."

"He is gnawing a bone," muttered Atanasio.

"Because," said Theophrastus, "long years in the care of Pedro Ruiz de Azagra made him revert to a bestial state. Next to him, in the same bottle, you may discern an even more tragic and pitiful figure: a man known as Harold Clatter. See him wag his tail!"

"That doesn't make sense. It's against the laws—"

"Of nature? Yes, of course. This is *supernature* and not all of it can be explained. But I don't wish to keep you longer than necessary. Consider a sweeter animal in the fourth bottle."

"It's a bird. A tropical bird," said Ignacio.

Theophrastus clapped his hands. "Quite right. A toucan! And yet it's a transformed man too. His name is Oroondates de Gris; he was a master of the magic arts, an alchemist of sorts; and in the fifth bottle we can see one of his pupils, a skilled dabbler named Gisberto, who accidentally invented the cliché while trying to make gold."

Atanasio sneered, "You are toying with us."

The sorcerer said. "I do not tell jokes. I have always been a sober man. Before I became a sorcerer I was—"

"What exactly *were* you?" frowned Ignacio.

"An astronomer. I made my own lenses, grinding for days on end. My telescopes were probably the best in the world at the time. Yes, I created one that was so powerful it could read a book on the moon! But how turn the pages? Impossible! So I abandoned that science for this art. I am glad I did so. Night work is exhausting!"

Atanasio gestured with his iron bar. "Who is this fellow in this bottle? He seems most eager to speak to us."

"Yes, he desires to tell you his tale. He is Iñigo Alfau."

"From which year comes he?"

Theophrastus tapped the glass, listened to the sound.

"1720, give or take a decade."

The figure in the bottle cried, "I could have told you that if you asked me, but nobody ever asks me anything! They just ignore me. Iñigo Alfau is a dullard, they say! Iñigo Alfau is fit only for looking after sheep! But I lusted after learning and higher things. I wanted to be a philosopher! Poor men aren't allowed to attend university and my ambitions were frustrated. Such great ideas I had! I knew how to thwart our enemies in Portugal but the authorities didn't care. Poison the Tajo, I said, at its source: for what is small as it crosses Spain becomes significant when it reaches Lisbon. But did they act on my advice? No!"

Ignacio and Atanasio leaned forward.

"His voice," they agreed, "is very faint, muffled by the thickness of the glass. We can only understand a few disjointed words of what he says. He appears agitated in the extreme."

Theophrastus pursed his lips and nodded.

Iñigo Alfau realised he was losing the attention of his visitors and with wild gesticulations he attempted to recapture their interest. "Wait! Listen to my theories about the universe! For instance, what are clouds? Clever men will talk about water vapour and cool steam, but they are blind, deaf, dumb. I know what clouds truly are! Sky sheep, that's what! Yes, they are sky sheep; the sun and moon are shepherd and shepherdess taking turns to watch over them; and the winds are loyal sheepdogs, flocking them first one way, then another! Sky sheep!"

"His ravings are disturbing me," said Atanasio.

"Even though I can't hear his words, the gyrations of his lips give me an uneasy feeling," added Ignacio.

Theophrastus Tautology smiled in sympathy.

"Come into the next room, where my fireplace is located. It's not really a fireplace but a boiler, a special one of my own devising. I also keep the Holy Grail there. As an ornament."

Ignacio and Atanasio almost fell into each other's arms.

"The Grail? A foul lie!"

The sorcerer widened his smile. "Come and see for yourself. It sits on top of my boiler; often I take a sip of herbal tea from it. Why tremble so? Do you have a chill, my friends?"

"The Grail is not here! The Grail is in Jerusalem!"

"Or in Naples! Or in Vienna!"

"Or in Athos! Or in Wallachia! Or in Scotland!"

"Or in Santiago! Or in Paris!"

Theophrastus raised his hand for quiet. "You are referring to the first one, but there's a second. It has been here in Albarracín ever since young Don Fernán watched it fall from a stork's beak. You wonder why two are necessary? The second was for a future god, already expected when Don Fernán fired his arrow at the bird."

"A second god? A rival? You blaspheme!"

"He came to this cosmos in the year 1499, one hundred and eighty six years after Don Fernán picked the second Grail up. But you don't need to worry too much about such things!"

"I demand proof of your words!" growled Atanasio.

"Follow!" said Theophrastus.

The he passed through the nearest door.

Full of trepidation, the two inquisitors went after him. They entered a room almost circular: in the centre was a curious boiler, a glass tank full of swirling mists connected to a chimney that speared upwards through a glass roof. Instead of belching fumes out of this chimney, the contraption seemed to be sucking them in from the air outside; and the pipes that ran into the mouths of the big bottles originated here. Something wasn't right about the arrangement. But what?

On top on the boiler rested a wooden cup.

Ignacio went down on his knees; Atanasio instantly berated him. The first inquisitor stood up quickly, but then the other had second thoughts and half bent his own knees. Ignacio clutched his head; Atanasio chewed his lower lip. The sorcerer enjoyed their confusion. Should they submit to this Grail or not? Everything in their training had conditioned them to fall down before relics of such power and divine grace; but they didn't know if it was appropriate in this instance.

"Heresy to do so, or not?" hissed Atanasio.

After a few minutes of observing their anguish, the sorcerer evidently decided he was satisfied and said:

"My poor guests, I must confess that I have tricked you. You came to drag me away in chains; and I wanted revenge for that presumption. But now I feel retribution is complete."

Ignacio was the first to recover. "What do you mean?"

Theophrastus stroked his chin.

"The Grail you see before you is an illusion. It's a congealed cloud in the shape of a cup, nothing more."

"A congealed cloud? What nonsense—"

The sorcerer held up his hand for silence and said, "It's a little known fact that clouds are sentient beings. They have a sense of humour too. The clouds that live above Albarracín are especially mischievous. Two of the most rascally decided to play an excellent joke on mankind. One took the form of a stork, another of a cup…"

Atanasio swung his iron. "Clouds have no substance. They cannot be touched or carried. You are a liar."

Theophrastus answered, "Congealed clouds have different properties to those of the expanded kind. Have you never felt a hailstone strike you on the head? These clouds played a joke on poor Don Fernán. Recently I made a pact with them; I promised them the opportunity to play an even greater joke on humans. They agreed to help me. I'm not a sorcerer at all, but merely an illusionist. Watch!"

And he pushed a lever attached to the boiler.

Hidden gears whined. The fumes stopped pouring into the tank. Now they began pouring out of it, through the chimney and back into the sky. Then Theophrastus laughed and said:

"I have put this machine into reverse. Say goodbye!"

"To whom?" wondered Atanasio.

"Why, to all the long-dead people you met in the other room! To the ambassador from Alpuente, to the English knight, to Louis the Wolf, to Harold Clatter, to Oroondates de Gris and Gisberto, and to Iñigo Alfau, the most neglected of all geniuses!"

And as he spoke those words, the personalities in question appeared in the glass pipes, horribly elongated, rushing into the glass tank and then up the chimney to reform themselves in their true shapes, as clouds floating serenely in the blue dome of the day.

Then he clapped his hands and the Grail itself dissolved, but as it was outside the tank it had to find its own way out of the glass house, floating down the corridor and passing through the keyhole of the fig wood door like a streamer of pipe smoke. Atanasio and Ignacio conferred together in whispers. Then they nodded forcefully.

"You wish to prove you aren't a sorcerer, that you can't raise the spirits of the dead, and that it was only the help of the clouds that permitted you to fool us in your obscure game—"

"That's perfectly correct," concurred Theophrastus.

"But," snarled Atanasio, "even an illusionist is a type of sorcerer, and anyone who plays tricks on the Inquisition is a species of heretic; and so you will burn at the stake anyway!"

"Your inclination to cruelty is regrettable."

Ignacio spluttered, "Cruelty? No, we are generous! We try to save the souls of the damned! That isn't cruel at all. True, our generosity isn't kind but it's no less generous for that!"

"I don't care for the unkind sort," said Theophrastus.

"A moot point," said Atanasio.

"Not really. The fact of the matter is that my trick isn't finished yet. I merely wanted to let you think, for a moment, you had won and that I was within your power. It's an example of my own generosity, the *kind* kind. I have some surprising news for you."

"What is it?" demanded Atanasio with a grimace.

Theophrastus took a step closer.

"The real Atanasio and Ignacio are still on their way here. They aren't yet more than a dozen leagues outside Toledo. Maybe the war is delaying their progress. By the time they reach Albarracín, I'll be long gone and so will this house. That's the truth."

"The real—? Then what are—?"

Theophrastus puffed out his cheeks and exhaled. The two inquisitors dissolved into yellowish fog, surface clouds that seethed and lapped like waves against the sorcerer's knees.

He flapped the ends of his cloak. The house dispersed.

The turquoise bricks expanded, became diffuse, wafted up into the sky and joined the other clouds there.

He was standing in an empty space.

The only thing that remained was the fig wood door.

That was real. That alone…

Theophrastus strode forward, caught it before it fell, tucked it beneath his arm. Then he walked off with it. He passed out of the environs of the city of Albarracín. Where he went next, nobody knows. An hour after he had vanished out of sight over a red hill, the other buildings of Albarracín started chattering to each other.

"He didn't realise that Napoleon's troops have already invaded Aragon and smashed this town to rubble!"

"There was nothing to be gained by upsetting him."

"Let's return into the sky!"

Like dreams or bubbles, these buildings burst softly, turning into mists that lifted upwards. Nothing was left of Albarracín; it had been destroyed. But a hidden spring now registered this fact. Contingency plans had been made long ago. Panels in the ground slid back. Houses that were perfect replicas of the originals rose into position. Albarracín was pristine again. The first spare had come in useful; and when the real inquisitors arrived, they would find nothing untoward.

Scaramouche's Pouting Mouth

He was the last clown still left alive after the battle. True, he had been the *only* clown involved in the action, at least the only professional one, but that didn't diminish to any noticeable degree the achievement in his own estimation. With the shrieking and pounding of the artillery shells fresh in his ears, he threw away his rifle and stumbled down the slope of the steep hill and into the darkening valley.

He ran for another hour without pausing.

Then he slowed his pace and allowed his arms to dangle loosely at his sides. His knapsack pulled at his shoulders awkwardly; he adjusted straps until he was comfortable again. But he didn't stop moving his legs, for he had to get away from the conflict zone, flee from the war and hatred. He'd had enough of hazarding his neck.

Deep in his soul he was still an anarchist; but his nerves were shredded to wisps no more substantial than the highest thinnest clouds. The thunder of the heavy guns had taken away his appetite for struggle. He was empty and scared. Was he a coward or simply a survivor? Maybe neither. Clown again, that was for certain, but only that? He wasn't sure. Lurching like an unstable flame, he hurried onwards.

It was black all around now, solid night.

Scaramouche they had called him, his comrades in arms, and he wasn't insulted by the nickname, for the original character had been cunning and wise as well as foolish and naïve. He wore tinted spectacles because of an old eye complaint and even knew some soft melodies on the guitar, which made a comparison with that wistful figure more accurate; but his talents were more varied than the buffoon's.

The local militiamen weren't familiar with the *commedia dell'arte* and didn't really understand the reference, but most of the Italian volunteers in the International Brigades knew and approved. Many of the enemy facing them in the stark Aragon hills were Italian volunteers too, and they called across to each other: sometimes curses, more often ironic greetings. Irony followed by real iron, by sharp bullets.

Scaramouche thought that if he could reach the French border it might be easy to slip across undetected and escape Spain altogether; Aragon and the other regions could fester under the Nationalist killers for all he cared. The war was lost. He was weary of politics, blood and treachery. But how far to the frontier? Weeks of travelling on blistered feet. He was certain to be caught. He needed a superior plan!

The moon rose over a distant peak and penetrated the foliage with one creamy beam; it fell on an old signpost by the side of the path. Worn with age, the stone letters were still legible in the pallid glow. Albarracín, only twenty kilometres. The name was familiar, but why? He remembered! A story his father once told him, the same father who had bequeathed all the tricks of his tumbling trade to his son.

Long before the son was born, his father, Pablo, had found himself in Albarracín on his way to a circus show in Teruel. Night was drawing on. Instead of finishing the journey at such a late hour, Pablo decided to rest here until dawn; he located an empty house, laid out his rug on the floor and curled up to sleep. The house was in a poor state of repair, had been abandoned by its owners for that reason.

All through the night, plaster dust fell from the crumbling ceiling; the upper joists of the house groaned alarmingly. Unable to relax, Pablo rose and went outside. No sooner did he step over the threshold than the house collapsed behind him! He was enveloped in a thick cloud of dust. When it eventually settled, Pablo was amazed to see that the house was still there, not only intact but in perfect condition!

A watchman appeared with a lantern, surveyed the scene and smiled at Pablo knowingly. "Yes, that's one peculiar feature of our town. Whenever a building is destroyed, an identical copy rises from the ground to replace it. Nobody recalls why this should be so; clearly there are spare copies of Albarracín existing beneath our feet."

The watchman departed and Pablo went inside the new house. Now he was able to sleep in safety and peace. The following morning, at dawn, he left for the tough walk to Teruel; and he never questioned the watchman's explanation. Scaramouche had never known his father to lie... And as the son continued towards Albarracín, fleeing from war and death, a cunning scheme fermented itself in his mind...

The twenty kilometres remaining to Albarracín were difficult. First the valley ended in a wall of stone, impassable; then the rocky path spiralled tightly to the summit of a mountain, twisted down the far side, up another peak, down again, and so on. But within a few hours he came to a narrow stream. This was the mighty Tajo! Thin enough to step over, an absurdity of geography! He crossed it like that.

His foot slipped on the muddy bank and he fell.

Into the stream. Into the icy froth!

It was deeper than he expected, much deeper. The rucksack dragged him down; his feet touched no bottom. The water closed over his gasping face. Down, down, he went. And as he fell, it seemed to him that versions of the same moonlit landscape flashed past. Impossible! Then he touched the riverbed, dragged himself to the bank, hauled himself up, gasping and spluttering like a dying humanoid eel.

He shivered, clenched his teeth. Nothing for it now but to resume his trek; at least exercise would warm him up. More mountains, more spiral paths. He progressed in this laborious fashion with painful lungs; and did not reach his destination until dawn, the same hour that his father had left it all those years earlier. Albarracín!

Rosy beams of the bloated sun on rosy cliffs and rosy towers, a magic quality to the light and air. He wandered the thin streets and thinner alleys until he reached the central *plaza*, and there he stopped and removed his rucksack with a sigh of relief and sat on it. There was bread and cheese in his pocket; he ate a welcome breakfast. His intended plan called for great daring. Did he have such daring? Yes!

The resolve of a clown must never be doubted.

He waited until the first stirrings of the general populace, the opening of the first shutter of a window. Then he stood and delved into his sack, removed what lay within. The contents were still dry, despite the sack's soaking in the Tajo, for they were wrapped in an oiled cloth. He extracted them one at a time, laid them out.

Sticks of awful power, the colour of clay!

He had been given them for safekeeping by the overall commander of his division. None had been used; the opportunity hadn't been there. They would be used now, for his own purposes. He selected three sticks, threw them high into the air, caught them.

He juggled in increasingly elaborate patterns.

Finally a voice hailed him: "Don't you know what those objects are? If you drop one, might it not explode?"

Without breaking his rhythm, Scaramouche said, "Yes, I am juggling with dynamite, but it's quite safe. I am a skilled performer. Summon your neighbours and friends here. I am going to put on a show for you, a show unlike any seen before! A marvel of marvels! Call all the fair inhabitants of Albarracín. Call them here now!"

He continued to juggle while feet pounded.

There was the murmuring of many voices and the clearing of several throats. Realising he had a sizeable audience, Scaramouche finished his juggling routine, turned his attention to the people. They stood watching him from the other edge of the *plaza*. He threw back his head and used a ringmaster's voice to address them:

"Good citizens of this lovely pink town! I don't care what side you are on in this dreadful war. Perhaps you are ardent for Franco! Maybe it's the Republicans you support! I don't care and I don't want to know. But I do wish to make a deal with you. These are my terms. If you are happy with the results of my coming performance, then you must pay me by hiding me among you and protecting me."

Before anyone could answer him, he took a breath and continued, "It no longer matters to me who wins, merely that I stay alive! When you see my show, you will consider my price a bargain! Look at the buildings that stand around you. All of them are crumbling, falling apart! But what if it was possible to replace them with undamaged copies of themselves? This refers not to restoration but rebirth!"

An objector shouted, "Houses can't be reborn."

"Incorrect!" roared Scaramouche.

"They are inanimate and unconscious; like clouds."

"Not so!" bellowed Scaramouche.

"Bricks have no regenerative properties at all."

"Nonsense!" hissed Scaramouche.

"Prove it to us, clown! Make it happen as you say."

"Is everyone here?" he asked.

"Indeed! The community is gathered in this place!"

"And all the houses are empty?"

"Yes. Every single one."

Scaramouche nodded. In his pocket was a box of matches also in oiled cloth, for men still smoke even when they fight in rain. He took one out, struck it on the sole of his right boot, lit the fuse of a stick, cast that stick through the window of a house.

"That's my property!" shouted someone.

The dynamite exploded. The house collapsed into a pile of rubble. The citizens gaped helplessly as Scaramouche lit the next fuse; again he cast a fizzing stick through another window. Another blast, another collapse. He repeated this action eight times.

Half the buildings that ringed the *plaza* had gone.

Scaramouche bowed elegantly.

"Before I deal with the others, we'll see what happens to these! Wait a minute and observe the result!"

The dust settled. He peered forward, smiling.

The citizens muttered angrily.

They pointed at him and he answered:

"I don't understand! Every time a building in Albarracín falls down, a new one rises to take its place!"

A voice more gruff than any of the others barked, "Who told you that, clown? Where did you hear it?"

Scaramouche blinked. "My father, who wasn't a liar!"

"He told you that, did he?"

The gruff voice belonged to a man in a tattered uniform. In one hand he held an antique Japanese rifle. This war was fought with a mishmash of weapons. It was a bric-a-brac conflict, a tangle of equipment from any other recent conflict anywhere.

"Yes, he told me," admitted Scaramouche.

"And where do the replacement buildings come from?" continued the gruff voice, as the face above the voice grimaced: the nostrils flaring, the eyebrows clashing like bayonets.

"From under the ground. From the next level down…"

"But this is the *lowest* level."

"Ah!" Scaramouche croaked. "Then you mean—"

"There are no buildings under this town; nothing beneath us other than the rock and magma of the planet. All the other Albarracíns are up *there*. Take a closer look at our sky…"

The clown did so, saw that the clouds were painted on. The sun was an ingenious lamp of special power.

"It seems I've put on a bad show," he said.

The gruff man slid a bullet into the breach of his rifle and slammed the bolt forward; then he took careful aim. "Just for your information, we are anarchists in this town. That's the side we are on. I want you to know that before you taste the crimson dust."

He pulled the trigger. And Scaramouche pouted.

Knossos in its Glory

We know that Knossos was a palace; that it contained a structure called a labyrinth in which one might lose oneself; but what of an entire city made of such labyrinths, many copies of the same labyrinth, all joined together? Do we know of that? Now we do!

Let it be told of how the past took over the future, one morning, after a strange accident; and of how that accident became almost inevitable from the moment that Mogul Xenon shook his fist at an assistant and thundered in his baritone voice, "I want real sets on this film, do you understand me! No synthetic images at all. None!"

It was the year 2049 AD. The world simmered.

In a desperate effort to diminish the effects of a global catastrophe that industry, poor waste management and greed had been hatching for two or more centuries, engineers had lately developed a new building material, a type of plastic that absorbed excess carbon dioxide, methane, sulphur and other proscribed gases directly out of the atmosphere. Towers of greenish material dominated every cityscape.

Architects were compelled by international law to incorporate this dull but beneficial substance into their plans for all forthcoming projects: they had no choice in the matter. The penalties for building in stone, brick and glass were severe. Consequently the character of every urban skyline had altered radically since the invention of the special plastic. The great cities of the civilised world were like chessboards on which were crammed too many ugly, towering sickly bishops.

Even towns and villages bristled with them.

The big film studios didn't care about this: if they wanted an historical film they relied on trickery, on digital simulations, and superimposed the real actors on the convincing but nonexistent backgrounds. No movie had been made 'on location' for nearly two decades anyway. Actors, like most workers on other career paths, saw no reason to travel physically: it was a nuisance, a waste of time. Commuting as a custom was extinct, as dead as dodos, tigers and books. Simple fact.

Actors knew the system worked better now. During the production of a movie, the set, whatever it was, came to *them*. That's how it was, how it must always be. But Mogul Xenon thought differently. His latest project was a mediaeval epic set in Transylvania, a tale about the Turks, Dacians, Magyars, Saxons and other races. His technicians had already designed a set for it, an electronic mirage of 15th Century Sighișoara, perfect in every detail, down to the species of lichen on the stones. The appropriate actors had been hired. Everything was ready.

But Mogul Xenon wasn't satisfied and called a halt to production. Into his presence scurried an assistant; and the all-powerful producer made the demand that nobody had expected to hear again. Indeed, the assistant was shocked; how could he not be? His name was Beltan. Beltan Braces. Not nice to be in his position at that time!

The Mogul repeated his demand. Beltan cried:

"Real sets for the film? But that's simply impossible! There's nowhere left that looks realistic enough. The plastic towers cannot be demolished and they are everywhere now. Every new building is of that material and the same stuff is also used to repair any old ones. The film will become a horrid farce if you insist on this point."

And from his expression it was obvious that Beltan was imagining the historical epic with the modern towers looming greenish in every frame, spoiling the effect of duels, romantic encounters, agitated crowd scenes, battles, assignations and poisonings.

Mogul Xenon was gracious enough to ignore the lack of reverence in the assistant's tone. "You are going to inform me, I presume, that a town of purely ancient appearance can't be found anywhere? Well, that was my assumption too: until yesterday…"

Beltan awaited the revelation. The Mogul poured himself a small glass of genuine brandy, gargled with the prohibitively expensive liquid, licked his lips and explained smoothly:

"One of my directors was flying over Iberia because he was needed in person for a meeting at headquarters. Something went wrong with one of his gyros and his disc slid off course. Instead of flying between Barcelona and Seville in a straight line, he drifted slightly northwards and crossed a region of Lower Aragon that's completely outside the orthodox routes. As he did so, he happened to look down."

"What did he see?" breathed Beltan Braces.

"A forgotten town! A lost city!"

"Without any plastic towers?" cried Beltan.

Mogul Xenon nodded his asymmetrical head, his big ears flapping like offended waiters' dishcloths as he did so. "Not a single tower! For reasons unknown, that town has escaped the decree! It's unsullied, I say! It has no Twenty First Century features at all!"

"But did the pilot get a fix on its position?"

"He did. He's not a fool."

"What else do you know about it?"

The Mogul grinned. "The city is named Albarracín and has a colourful history, a tradition of independence."

Beltan asked, "Do you think it could be used as a convincing replica of Sighişoara? Is that what you mean?"

Mogul Xenon continued grinning. "Yes!"

"And also as a convincing replica of every other medieval town in any other historical epic we might make?"

"Yes again! For *all* of them, it's the perfect set!"

"You plan to buy Albarracín?"

"I already did! One hour ago."

"A story set in Transylvania filmed in Spain? It's not beyond reason in principle; but how will you persuade the actors to travel so far? They will cite the inviolable clause in their contracts that protects them from going anywhere at all. It's a point of honour for them; and if they go on strike it could endanger all our projects."

Mogul Xenon said, "I don't want more trouble than I can handle. Let's bring the set to them, as we always do. I see no reason to change that. We won't break any contracts at all."

"You want to dismantle Albarracín and cart it here?"

"No, I have a better idea."

Beltan waited for it. Mogul Xenon took another gulp of brandy, rolled his eyes and finally swallowed.

He said, "Put the city on wheels. On *wheels*."

"On wheels?" gasped Beltan.

"With solar-powered generators to drive them! And circuitry to guide the buildings along the roads. Now that nobody owns a car, the roads are practically empty. Each building could be given its own set of wheels and a miniature fake brain linked to the brains of the other buildings: with one central processor. No need for a human driver or navigator! We program a destination into the processor and wait for Albarracín to arrive under its own steam. Think of the benefits!"

Beltan counted them on his fingers. "Superior authenticity of backdrop and ambience, reduced workload on overstressed simulators, smaller risk of on-set interference from solar storms, hackers, digital espionage. Yes, I can see the appeal. It's a great idea."

Mogul Xenon regarded his assistant critically.

"That's not just flattery, is it? I want a lackey willing to say 'no' to my face even if it costs him his job—"

Beltan Braces drew himself up, angled his chin heroically. "You are a genius, sir. That's the plain *truth*."

Mogul Xenon dismissed him with a jolly wave.

"A portable town!" he giggled.

That's exactly what he got. Albarracín was put on wheels, given many tiny brains and a central nervous system. Subsequently, it trundled itself up and down the network of empty roads and delivered itself safely to the location where the actors resided.

The film about Transylvania was a success.

Other historical epics followed.

Albarracín was used to mimic dozens of ancient towns in many sectors of Europe. Often the illusion was very good, sometimes perfect. True, the occasional member of certain audiences quibbled with the accuracy of the background in special instances. A rose-red Spanish city pretending to be a fortress town in Albania or a Teutonic Knights outpost! But no one paid too much attention to such pedants.

The critics were rapturous about the innovation.

The fans were utterly enthralled.

Mogul Xenon became even richer and grosser than he already was. He was the man responsible for bringing historical epics back into fashion in the biggest imaginable way… Albarracín was booked ahead for the next five years. A complex schedule was inserted in the town's artificial mind. Back and forth across the continent it trundled, back and forth, first north, then south, east, west, fulfilling its programmed obligations. As for those who had lived in the city… Too bad.

The inhabitants of Albarracín were relocated.

Mogul Xenon owned the place. He could do anything he liked with it. Ruthlessness was something he was good at. He even prosecuted the few thrill-seeking individuals who hitched a ride in the houses as they passed, although this didn't deter them. Many died in the attempt to jump onto the speeding city anyway. And if they survived, they were arrested at the next destination. Youthful daredevils.

This story is almost over already. It's a myth from the future, though it will be exactly contemporary one day; and myths and legends from ahead do tend to be shorter and more concise than those from behind… So let it be told how Mogul Xenon summoned his assistant for an emergency talk that was less triumphant than the one previously described. Beltan Braces found his boss shaking with raw fury.

"Can you believe it? Can you credit the impudence?"

"I don't know yet," said Beltan.

The Mogul expounded his rage in these terms: "One of our numerous rivals has managed to get its hands on an Albarracín of its own! How did it accomplish that? I spoke to the chief of that studio, Mogul Neon, and I threatened legal action, but he just laughed at me; and he has put his own Albarracín on powered wheels too!"

"Surely an inferior copy?" suggested Beltan.

"By no means! There are no cardboard bricks involved. It's no less real and solid than our original version!"

"What do you plan to do?" wondered Beltan.

"Nothing, nothing! My lawyers tell me that a city can't be copyrighted. There's nothing to stop Mogul Neon making his own historical epics with his own Albarracín! What a disaster!"

It was. He was right about that.

In fact the situation soon grew much worse.

The chief of *every* other major film studio got his hands on Albarracín and fitted it with wheels and brains. 100 studios, 100 Moguls, 100 towns. But the hundredth was a slightly damaged version with half the buildings in its central *plaza* reduced to rubble. The studio that owned that one was resourceful enough to specialise only in historical *wartime* epics. Actors coughed in the dust of real debris…

"Where are they getting these extra Albarracíns from?" fretted Mogul Xenon; he despatched Beltan to find the answer. Beltan returned with the sad look of a man forced to travel.

"I believe I have found out," he declared.

"Tell me!" hissed the Mogul.

"A few moments after *your* Albarracín rolled away on its wheels, the second one rose up from the ground. Hidden springs and levers. Mogul Neon got his hands on that one. After *his* rolled away, the third one rose up; and then the fourth and fifth."

"Moguls Radon, Zinc and Curium got those!"

"Then the sixth, seventh, eighth, ninth, tenth, eleventh… All identical and all mounted on large wheels."

"How many more can we expect?"

"It seems that the hundredth was the last. After that one trundled off, nothing new came out of the ground. Engineers will probably blast a hole at the location to determine why."

"Too many Albarracíns! You're finished!"

"But it wasn't my fault—"

Mogul Xenon growled, "When the first assistant is trundled away, the second appears to take his place; and when the second also goes away, a third arrives, and so on. Where do these replacements all come from? It's a mystery! Get out of my sight!"

Beltan went. Now let's hear the proper end.

One hundred century-drenched cities rolling in elaborate patterns over the surface of Europe. A temptation for destiny too great to resist? Plainly fate has a sense of humour; that can't be doubted now. One evening in the centre of the landmass, at a point where all the roads came together in one junction, the Albarracíns collided. All of them. Collided and meshed into a single vast, complex metropolis.

Narrow alleys joined with other narrow alleys, knotted themselves into tangles that no one would ever untie. Staircases too. *Plazas* within *plazas*. Not a normal city but a labyrinth…

Go there and see for yourself if you don't believe!

Once you enter you can't leave.

Knossos has come back intact to the world.

A hundred Albarracíns equals one Knossos. That's the formula. Maze of mazes, full of souls already lost.

Join them; and whenever you find yourself in an open space, look up. High above the mass of seekers, the clouds still go about their business, seemingly oblivious to events below.

Author's Note:

The original edition of *Sangria in the Sangraal* ended here.
For this second edition I wrote and added the following two
new stories...

Señor Chimera's Hysterical History

He lived at the centre of the labyrinth and when he was bored he wrote poetry. It was bad verse and he felt sorry for it, as the powerful should when confronted with anything poor, and his large tears fell onto it and obliterated the words entirely or merely changed them, sometimes even improving the quality of the work but not by much. Generally he wrote his lyrics on old parchments in faded ink with quill pens fashioned from the feathers plucked from the mummified stork he found stuck in a chimney; on other occasions he composed it in the dust on the furniture with a thick finger as he roamed the house he called home.

He could have chosen any number of buildings in which to lurk, but he liked the fact he was stationed at the probable middle of the maze, not so much the heart of the tangle, for hearts are rarely at the centre of anything, but the stone, core, pip, the part that would remain when all the rest was systematically peeled away by the decaying teeth of time. The house he had selected was well stocked with interesting items; he passed delighted hours rummaging through the cupboards in the rooms or venturing into the attic or down into the cellar. If he couldn't locate what he wanted he sometimes broke into neighbouring houses.

But he always returned before nightfall to his own and refused to sleep on a bed that was unfamiliar to him. He was insular.

In the outer world, great changes were taking place.

The only time he learned of them, however, was when he received a visitor. He preferred to think of those lost souls who came to him as guests rather than as sacrifices, despite the evidence to the contrary.

"So time travel is normal now?"

"Yes, for history students; but it is rigidly controlled."

"And men can fly through space?"

"This is the last day of the 21st Century and colonies have been established on Mars by humans and on Titan by robots."

"That means almost nothing to me, I'm afraid."

"What are you afraid of?"

"Very little. It is your task to be afraid of me."

"True, for you are a monster."

"So they say. I don't feel like one, to be honest, but who am I to argue? It is said that a monster rarely believes he is one; and the fact I doubt my own condition is evidence to suggest the rumours are true."

"Oh, they are much more than rumours. Do you never look in a mirror, Señor Chimera? Or failing that, a shiny spoon?"

"The reflective surfaces here are all tarnished; but yes I often see myself in a puddle of rainwater and I know I have many faces. No man should have more than his share, which is one, a single face; and yet I have many of them, all looking in a different direction, seeing and believing."

"That is why they call you Señor Chimera, *amigo*."

"Yes, it is. I don't mind the name."

"But it's not strictly accurate. I mean, the original classical chimera had three heads and no more than that. Is it true you are a poet? Will you recite some of your verse before you eat me? I would enjoy that—"

Not all his guests are quite so amiable, but most are. Those few who struggle or seek to flee are the ones he dreads most; they disturb him, make it impossible for him to sleep later. There are many pillows on his bed, positioned at strange angles, one for each of his heads. If only other food was available he would never have any crises of conscience, but it rotted away in the pantries decades ago, even the tinned fruits are inedible now, and he doesn't know how to grow his own. He relies utterly on his guests; he is a host who is also a parasite.

If he climbs onto the roof of his house and stands on tiptoe, he can just see a portion of the sky that is crossed by aircraft on a regular basis. The aerial routes are rigid and Knossos lies outside them. He is surrounded on all sides by buildings and the streets of the maze, one hundred little cities jammed together haphazardly, the result of a collision that he still suspects left echoes in the stones of the walls, faint vibrations of inorganic trauma no less emotional than that suffered by living beings. The entire labyrinth thrums weakly but insistently.

There are days when he does nothing but listen to that vibration or employs it as musical accompaniment to his efforts to recall his early life. He has no memories of any childhood. There was nothingness and then suddenly he existed and he was already an adult and standing in a remote landscape of low rosy mountains and men were digging enormous holes in the ground with machinery near him. He wandered over to them and they fled, abandoning the tractors and cranes and grabbers. On the edge of the hole he stood and peered down into—

Blackness. There was nothing there, just shadows and echoes.

Into the chasm he kicked smooth pebbles.

He clambered playfully over the excavation machines, tested the hatches and windows, but was unable to enter any of them and lost interest; then he sat down in the irregular shade of the biggest crane and wondered what he was. A jaw opened and closed behind him, the emerging voice tugging at his numerous earlobes like a fistful of identical pegs, clamping his attention and hanging it out to dry. It was the foreman of the gang, who had refused to escape, knowing it was his responsibility to protect all the equipment, even from monsters.

"What are you doing here, O thing with many heads?"

"I don't know where 'here' is..."

"This is where the city of Albarracín once stood. As you can see, it has gone now, but it still exists elsewhere in a different, multiplied form. They have given it a new name and the unmapped layout of the streets is so confusing that once a man enters, he will probably never leave, unless he cheats with muddy footprints that he can follow back or uses satellite navigational tools. I've heard tales of young lovers wandering into it to look for solitude, only to remain inside forever; and presumably their bones now litter this *plaza* or that *plaza* or one of the other identical *plazas*. So it goes. But as for why you are here: I have no idea."

"Nor me. I am brand new, I think."

"Perhaps you spontaneously germinated from the soil."

"Is that likely? I am hungry."

"There is no food here. Lunchtime is over."

"My noses tell me that *you* are food. Forgive me for this."

"No, I will forget but never forgive."

And that was his first taste of dinner, his first sacrifice or guest, and he never even learned the name of the foreman who had foolishly remained behind to protect the equipment. When the chewing, which was shared between a great many mouths and had a weird polyrhythmic chatter to it, was finished, he wandered away. North he went, keeping the sun out of most of his faces, up a track to the top of a hill and down the far side. The landscape was ancient, serene, isolated but not quite lonely; and it was rosy, like the cheeks of a healthy cliché.

His own cheeks were flushed too, many of them, with the exertion. Onwards he kept going, until the sun went down and night came; and he tramped all through the night until dawn. At last he spied a distant figure coming towards him. It was a tall man with a vast net on a very long pole, and when he was within hearing range, he cupped his free hand to his mouth and bellowed:

"Are you the monster?"

"Yes, I must be. What do you want?"

"To catch you and render you harmless. I have been sent by the authorities to net you alive and convey you to an escape-proof holding pen until a final decision is reached regarding your ultimate fate."

"You know what I did to the foreman back there?"

"Indeed. We have been monitoring you from afar with telescopes. The world has become a relatively peaceful place; there is no room in it for monsters. I guess you will have to be disposed of. Let's see."

"I will resist the net. I am stronger than you are."

"The strands are electrified. Behold."

And he swung the pole around his head, whooshing the net in a bewildering pattern that was hypnotic. The monster was unable to move; he watched entranced as the finely woven wires came nearer and nearer on each revolution. Then he was suddenly inside the net, stunned as the current flowed into him and convulsed him into exhaustion and unconsciousness. The monster catcher was clearly an expert at his trade, though how often he was called upon to perform by the authorities is an intriguing question, unanswerable with present data.

The captive monster was shunted around the regional capitals of Europe and while in a variety of prisons he acquired an education and his name. Señor Chimera enjoyed classical poetry and baroque music; he was fed intravenously but it became clear that human beings were the only nourishment guaranteed to keep him fit. This was a problem. The authorities debated his destiny: some experts were keen to see him put down, not with a volley of insults but with depleted uranium bullets, while others thought he might be used in medical research.

The arguments went back and forth in public courts and in backrooms, in the media and in the chambers of secret committees.

There was no official precedent for such a situation.

Having materialised in Aragon seemingly out of thin air, some commentators were of the opinion he was legally the concern of that region's government only, or failing that, the responsibility of the Spanish *Cortes*; but Europe had altered far too much in the past century for such simple measures to suffice. There were no longer such things are purely local issues. All the countries of the continent were bound by the knots of intricate laws into a confederacy that was both mutually supportive and mutually interfering. No judicial decision was easy.

Months passed; and the months would inevitably turn into years and the case would end up costing a spectacular amount of money and effort that might better be concentrated elsewhere; and all because a monster had arrived from nowhere in one of the most obscure corners of the European mainland! To the average taxpayer this didn't seem fair. Why should they dip into their threadbare pockets in order to fund the permanent existence in legal limbo of a being with more heads than a scattering of tossed coins? The same coins taxed out of them...

That clumsy self-referential metaphor shouldn't distract from the fact that the people were furious. It wasn't as if the monster was doing anything useful with his extra heads, solving difficult mathematical problems such as devising a set with a cardinality larger than $\aleph_2$ or finding a consistent regular pattern in π or similar tasks worthy of the year, which was the most modern it could be. He wrote poetry, true, but that's archaic and not shiny enough. The people protested and marched through the streets, demanding that Señor Chimera be exiled.

He was fed on unclaimed bodies from sundry morgues but public anger grew even fiercer when this fact became common knowledge;

the authorities had to issue and process consent forms similar to those permitting organ transfers after death. At last, exasperated by the riots taking place nearly every day on the boulevards of the major population centres, the authorities reached a rare consensus. They announced that the problem was solved; the citizens merely had to wait for their solution to be implemented. In the meantime, go home and be calm.

Here is what happened. To liquidate him would expose the authorities to the risk of ruinous litigation if any of the monster's hypothetical relatives ever appeared in the future; and yet he couldn't be kept in prison because of the expense. So exile was indeed the wisest option, and a junior clerk suggested the perfect place to send him to. Knossos. That labyrinth of twisted alleyways and superimposed plazas, that maze designed by collision and not by any sane or insane mind. They dragged him to the outskirts and released him there. "In you go!"

"Indigo? I see no such colour."

"You are stalling for time with word games."

"I genuinely misheard you."

"In you go! Not indigo! Hurry, hurry."

"Is there food for me inside?"

"Don't worry. You'll be provided for."

But he was still reluctant to enter the maze; so they urged him on with steel ball bearings projected at speed from powerful handheld catapults, and so he began his long loneliness. He had intended to stay close to the edge, so he might leave at his own discretion whenever he chose, establishing his base at a point a few streets deep and no more; but the wonder of the wandering made him forget this resolution and he kept going from the shadows of the thin streets to the sudden brightness of a *plaza*, back into the shadows. It was an odd delight.

And so he came to the centre, almost as if tugged there by gravity, and broke the lock of a door and went inside a house; and immediately the house became his, a minor palace for a minotaur who wasn't really a minotaur or even a chimera but a brand new kind of awfulness. Knossos, his home and doom. A hundred Albarracíns in a nightmare of quaintness and picturesque decay.

That was Señor Chimera's history.

He found it hysterical in both senses of the word.

And since then he has dwelled in the labyrinth, both a prisoner and demigod, a rumoured curiosity and a sidelined menace.

The sacrifices come to him irregularly. They are nearly always students who have failed their exams and wish to commit suicide. They make an inverse perverse pilgrimage to Knossos and take deep breaths on the edge of the tangle; then either they boldly plunge into it or timidly turn and go home. For those who enter there is rarely any escape other than through death when they finally meet the monster and generally they are glad to do so. The few reluctant ones are those who change their injured minds when they see him for the first time.

It is not a legal procedure, of course, but the authorities knew from the outset it would happen and they turn a blind eye. How can one ban suicide? They are only really interested in forgetting about the monster as much as possible. There is work to do and he is a distraction. The future is clanking and grinding along, not running as smoothly as it should; nobody knows why this might be so. Space stations, robot doctors, farmscrapers, hovertrains, elevated walkways, triple lifespans: they are all in place but utopia still seems no closer than before.

Señor Chimera isn't part of it, has no place in a shiny world. He is a hideous anomaly, a throwback or some sort of *throwsideways*, which is worse. Left alone in the labyrinth, he is safely out of sight and thought.

Again he hears the sound of footsteps and gazes down from his vantage into the streets nearest his home. Someone appears from around a corner. A woman. For several minutes he observes her as she approaches the most central *plaza* of all the *plazas*, the one below his house. Then he stretches his body and climbs down from the roof to greet her. He opens his front door and steps through it, easing his oddly shaped and enormous form into a dusty sunbeam.

"Here I am," he announces.

She turns her head, frowns and approaches him.

He is staggered by such confidence. Normally they are much less direct and even those who are very keen to be leave life require coaxing; but not this one. She is smiling broadly and extending a hand in greeting. He has never shaken a human hand before and does not care to start now. He takes a step backwards and collides with the door, which has swung shut on its own.

"You seem ill at ease today."

"That is the case every day. I am insular."

She smiles. "I am Ursula."

"That is similar, but it is not the same," he says.

"Should it be? Why so?"

"Then you are my latest guest?"

"Not necessarily. Listen carefully. I have come here to offer you something. This offer must be kept secret. It's a thesis."

"Theseus? Yes, he slew the Minotaur, but I am a chimera."

"You are not even that. And yet—"

"I misheard you, didn't I?"

She nods. He notices for the first time that she is carrying a large suitcase. Is she planning to move in with him and live in Knossos permanently? What a curious notion! She says, "You have too many ears."

"And that is why I tend to mishear things, is it?"

"You heard me correctly. Yes."

He rubs one of his many chins in bafflement. "You don't want to be eaten? I eat people whether they desire it or not."

"I hope you will permit me to make my offer first."

"This is highly irregular."

"Not as irregular as you are, surely?"

"True. Very well. Please say what you came to say."

"Thank you, Señor Chimera."

Ursula puts down her suitcase and sits on it, legs extended, rubbing her eyes. It has been a long journey through the knot of streets and she would prefer to sleep before explaining, but there is no time for that.

"Some of us in academia are troubled by the present situation that pertains. It seems a tragic waste that so many promising young men and women choose to die in this labyrinth rather than continue their studies. Clearly there are complex issues involved and we can't expect to solve all of them, but there is one factor we *do* feel we can do something about. You. We want you to stop eating students. We know it is pointless asking you to go against your nature, so we've devised a plan. We are willing to offer you the use of a time machine..."

"What for? To travel through time, clearly, but what for really?"

"To get rid of you. To free you from the labyrinth. To liberate the Minotaur without having to lead him out the slow way."

"Why should I go? I like it here."

"We are asking you politely." She taps the suitcase that is her seat with her knuckles. "The device is inside and can be utilised immediately. This is an illegal offer, I must remind you. The controls have been set for the Upper Palaeolithic, where there will be many early humans to worship you, if you can make yourself a deity among them. They will undoubtedly offer sacrifices to you on a daily basis. This seems more ethical than feeding intelligent students to you, although it does raise certain difficult moral questions of its own."

"Knossos is my home but—"

"You will enjoy yourself much more back then."

"Yes, I will go. I have been waiting for this offer all my life without realising it. I will go and settle there in dim prehistory."

"It's good that you are so understanding about it."

"How will *you* leave the labyrinth?"

"I won't. But that's no problem because I'm not really here. I'm a robot. My mission consists of several parts and the first was to put the proposal to you. If you refused I would have opened the case and pressed a button on the machine and sent it back to a period before the planet had even coalesced. When you go I will remain here and when despairing students turn up I will teach them. They won't find death in the maze but continued education. And so Knossos will become a university and all the buildings will be classrooms and dorms."

"That is an ambitious scheme."

"Indeed. Within a few years Knossos College will be the prime educational establishment in Europe! I am a messenger, courier and lecturer. I have delivered the message and now the machine is yours."

"What if I had tried to eat you before giving you a chance to speak? Would I have choked on cogs and electronic components?"

"No, I am a meat robot."

"Edible, you mean? What if I eat you anyway?"

"The moment the flesh is bitten off my bones, a new Ursula would pop into existence; and once that one was eaten, a third Ursula would appear, and so on, ad infinitum. The method was learned from studying the site of the original Albarracín. They dug deep to discover the secret of its renewal, found that secret and adapted and miniaturised it. I embody the principle. If you had declined to journey into the past, student lives still would be saved. You could dine instead on me forever. I am almost indestructible. Now I suggest we say—"

"Farewell? Yes, I am ready."

"Me too." Ursula stands and turns to bend down and open the suitcase. The gleam of chrome within blinds many of his eyes for an instant. Will there be poetry in the Palaeolithic? Perhaps not but he can always introduce it. He pictures himself on the summit of a hill, surrounded by his devotees, burning torches thrust into the sacred ground, the air filled with the chanting of his latest doggerel as he declaims with all his mouths simultaneously, a primitive labyrinth made of sonic corners and dead ends. Then his mind snaps to the present.

"Will you erect a statue of me? In your college. I know that universities often have statues of famous alumni and worthies."

"But you haven't graduated..."

"Without my agreement the college wouldn't be possible. I deserve a statue. I am a benefactor of sorts, that's a fact."

Ursula inspects him from head to toes, from his other heads to his other toes, and finally she shrugs with a wistful smile.

"If we can find enough raw materials," she says.

The Bone Throwers

It was the morning of August 6th in the year 20,307 BC but nobody knew it. They didn't use those sorts of dates back then. Nonetheless that's when what happened actually happened, just in case you ever need to set the controls of a time machine and check for yourself. I don't recommend it.

The sun had risen an hour before.

Og climbed the slope towards the dead god.

His shoes, woven from twigs, were like two ungainly birds' nests jammed onto the ends of his legs, but they were comfortable and provided the perfect grip necessary to climb slippery hills. It had rained all night and the mud oozed under him like the thick gravy of a butchered liver.

He was going to claim the final hunk of meat.

Ever since the god had turned up, eight months previously, his people had feasted well on the divine flesh. The god had spoken a strange language but with his many arms and grimaces he had been able to communicate with gestures. The god was keen to convey the idea of 'sacrifice' and Og's tribe had responded with extreme bawling enthusiasm to this suggestion.

They rushed at the god with flint knives gleaming.

And so now the god was dead.

It stood on the summit of the rosy hill, a bizarre skeleton, vast and strange and intimidating, but no more so to Og than many other aspects of the world: the moon, the thunder, the bears. Everything was natural to him and nature itself was supernatural. The god's skeleton simply was what it was; he was frightened of it, yes, but he was also prepared to fight that fear.

There was no discernible symmetry to the network of bones, and the shadow of the entire frame shifted to create new patterns too intricate for the mind of Og as the sun lifted higher over the deserted mountains and valleys. One day Albarracín would exist at this very spot, and history would roam its narrow alleyways dressed in turbans and armour and various other guises.

But not now, not yet... History was still fast asleep.

The god, as we already know, had come from the future, from a place known as Knossos, thanks to a time machine small enough to fit inside a suitcase, hugging it to one of his chests as he spiralled back through the chronoflow. He arrived in an unpleasant place, a swamp, and decided to pick his way out to firmer ground. With discordant slurps he waded to freedom, wryly musing to himself on the similarities between a swamp and a maze, his noses twitching.

Then on a whim he decided to find the location of Albarracín even though he knew there would be nothing there. How would he recognise the site when he reached it? He felt sure he could but he couldn't say why. Some sort of aura about the place, some kind of mental or spiritual energy.

And so he tramped a continent without smooth roads, with only tracks that never went in straight lines, and he awed and terrified the few people who watched his passing from afar; and none of them chucked a spear at him and this gave him a false confidence, the swagger of a god among men.

Many months later he knew he was at his destination. The mountain range, the Sierra de Albarracín, was slightly different, but not by much. The source of the Tajo was in almost exactly the same spot. Yes, this was his rightful home, thus he climbed a hill to the north of the non-existent city and established himself there at the crown and waited patiently to be worshipped.

Within days, the bravest men of Og's tribe were clustering at the base of the hill; then gradually they began to ascend it, a little higher each time, until finally a formal meeting took place. Then the other men, the women and children also came to pay their respects to this curious hideous figure.

He was hungry, famished in fact, and he pointed at many of his mouths with many of his fingers and patted many of his stomachs with many of his other hands and he spoke to them in verse; but they understood not a word of that. They shook their heads in wonderment. Hunger! Yes, they were hungry; and the god seemed to be offering himself to them. Is that what he meant?

It must be. That was the best interpretation. This god had come to stuff their bellies with the holy meat wrapped on his bones.

Divine generosity indeed!

It would have been uncouth to refuse such an offer.

And so they slaughtered him...

Despite his strength and agility, he was no match for fifty fit warriors and he died very quickly, each heart extinguished almost at the same time as the others. It was the end of his daydream; the burning torches thrust in the ground, the chanting crowds with the words of his poetry in their mouths...

His dream had rubbed up against their need; and the need won.

The tribe dined on him richly.

Everyone benefitted, even the weakest.

And now it all was gone, all save one single piece.

Og had been chosen to fetch it because it was *his* turn. The hunk was for him and no other. The reason for this was simple.

It was his birthday. For Og's a jolly good fellow.

Three cheers! Hip hip wraugggh!

Og reached the top of the slope. He paused to rest by leaning against one of the god's shinbones, catching his breath in deep grateful gulps. Then he heard the snickering of an intruder. He jerked alert and—

Ug was facing him, steaming meat in one hairy hand.

The thief! The dirty sneaky thief!

Og was shocked. He knew that Ug was rapacious, as were they all, but never had he expected him to violate the birthday tradition. And yet why had he allowed himself to be caught in the act like this?

Clearly Ug wanted a fight, a struggle, a bashing.

"Mugawrrh!" growled Og, pointing a dirty and callused finger at Ug, who responded with a defiant, "Raughhrr!"

These were not the words of a real language but sounds that accompanied a basic set of emotions and actions. They were imprecise and had to be paired with an expression or gesture to have meaning. The birth of an authentic tongue for this tribe hadn't come yet but was imminent.

"Krgghsshhrrrggghshgsrrghshh!" retorted Og.

"Ngrhshhgrhh?" countered Ug.

"Jjghhrsbbghhrhhrrgghhh!" insisted Og.

"Srauughhrh?" mocked Ug.

"Prgghhshhhhhgsrrrr!" retaliated Og.

"Furgghh?" queried Ug.

"Mrrr!" screamed Og and that settled it.

They had to fight now. There was no other choice. A battle in the shadow of the god, or rather in front of the god, for the shadow was on the far side. They were between it and the sun, and somehow that felt right, dramatic, important. But they were both without weapons. Because this was the last piece of flesh there had been no need to cut it from the bone; simply, to reach and grab was enough. Neither Og nor Ug had a flint knife with them. What to do?

Og's left hand still touched the shinbone of the god. His closed his fingers in a powerful grip, tugged and the bone came free.

He brandished it like a club, a white weapon of divine justice!

The skeleton didn't topple. There were too many other legs holding it up; but the gap was uncanny, unnatural, and Og moved away from it. He approached Ug in a murderous curve, swinging the bone in two hands and bringing it down as hard as he could on the crown of Ug's unwholesome head. Ug blinked and coughed and his knees bent to absorb the impact. The sound was a single huge clack! It was as if an ancient tree had abruptly snapped in the middle.

To express his triumph, Og threw the bone up into the air. He expected it to soar high, turning end over end, pause like a tourist at the highest point of the flight to admire the view, and then spin all the way back down and land near his feet. He might even catch it if he was lucky; but it didn't do that. No. It went up and up, and yes, it did rotate on its own axis, but at the apex of its trajectory it turned into some other object and sped away. Og was bewildered.

Ug took the opportunity of this distraction to approach the god and wrench a bone of his own off the bizarre frame. He swung it around and around in a circle. If his tribe had learned to count higher than seven he would have described a figure of eight with it, but they hadn't. He bashed the end down on Og's cranium with nearly the totality of his strength. Og gasped and sighed.

Then Ug threw his own bone into the air and it too underwent the extremely illogical transformation. It paused at the highest point of its spin, turned into a long object that wasn't a bone and sailed off through the sky. They observed it together until it had dwindled to nothing. Now it was Og's turn to pick off a bone and slam it down on Ug's head and toss it into the empyrean.

And that's how the morning proceeded. Bones yanked off the skeleton of the increasingly impoverished god; employed as a club to smite a foe; and then, with a flick of a hairy wrist, the weapon launched heavenwards in victory only to alter and slide away and vanish, as if into the future. But the future for Og and Ug wasn't the world you and I know and appreciate but merely another day like all other days, the pattern of tribal existence repeated again and again.

Ug chose a bone with care and cracked Og over the skull.

Og did the same to Ug. So it went.

There were hundreds of bones on the skeleton and at some point a vital strut was finally removed and the remaining lattice collapsed onto them, saving them the effort of beating each other. They capered among the white ruins, hefting up bones and throwing them into the sky, watching them go.

Even the skulls were projected upwards; and they too changed and vanished. And finally there was nothing left, no more bones of any sort, just Og and Ug with blood streaming over their grimacing faces, their immensely hard heads still intact but their brawny arms weary with all the exercise. So they sat together, craned back their necks and peered at the sky and Og spoke.

He spoke the first genuine word any member of his tribe had ever uttered. It was a word that would form the basis of the original language of Albarracín. As the last flying bone slid into eternity, the word came.

"Spaceship!" he croaked.

Ug considered this and nodded. "Spaceship!"

"Spaceship!" chortled Og.

Ug clutched his stomach in mirth. "Spaceship!"

"Spaceship! Spaceship!"

Neither of them had any idea what a spaceship was, they didn't even have a concept of space or a ship, but they felt that *spaceship* was the right word to apply to what those bones had turned into in the sky.

And so they became friends.

As for the spaceships, they were clouds...

This is how it was... When the final Albarracín had rolled away on wheels to serve as a film set for some movie mogul, many of the clouds present had left with the city but others had stayed. Those who declined to go were convinced that their home was in the place where Albarracín had *stood*, rather than above the buildings themselves. These clouds, the ones that remained, guarded the site jealously; when men came with mechanical diggers to spoil it—

Well, the clouds had held a conference to work out what they could do about the intolerable situation. They decided to amalgamate themselves into a single foul being, a monster, and to frighten the workers away. But the moment they formed a gestalt they lost their individual identities and thus their memories. Señor Chimera was a brand new being, as far as he was concerned, and he forgot that he was made from clouds. He lived the fiction, the myth, the lie.

But now the clouds had been liberated once more, thanks to the dismantling efforts of Og and Ug. The bones of the skeleton were tightly-rolled cumulus, cirrus and nacreous clouds, and they fled their cramp like cigar-shaped objects and slowly unrolled themselves back into fluffiness or wispiness. As for the flesh on the bones of Señor Chimera, that was a chewy combination of mud, congealed fog, borrowed meat taken from the students he had devoured.

Just a typical misunderstanding.

Og and Ug thought they could hear music.

Also Sprach Albarracín.

Lightning Source UK Ltd.
Milton Keynes UK
UKHW010633271120
374167UK00002B/70/J